Escape from the Shadows
A Novel

Sequel to

Escape from the Belfry

Escape from the Shadows
A Novel

Doris Gaines Rapp

Sequel to
Escape from the Belfry

Daniel's House Publishing

Copyright © 2017 by Doris Gaines Rapp

Daniel's House Publishing
P.O. Box 623
Huntington, Indiana 46750

This book is a work of fiction. Names, characters, places and incidents are either products of the author's imagination or used fictitiously. Any resemblance to actual events, locales or persons, living or dead, is entirely coincidental.

Keystone Avenue—a real name—and several other streets in Beavertown, were re-named some years after 1946.

For information contact: Daniel's House Publishing at: www.danielshousepublishing@gmail.com

Beavertown E.U.B. Church window: Photographer unknown.
Map art on page five by Mary Coons, marycoonsdesigns.com

Certain stock imagery: hummingbird on cover © Shutterstock.com and the "painting" © Dreamstime.com

Library of Congress Control Number: 2017901613
ISBN: 978-0-692-84229-4 (paperback)
ISBN: (eBook – available: Amazon, BN.com, and other sites)

Contact Daniel's House Publishing at
www.danielshousepublishing@gmail.com

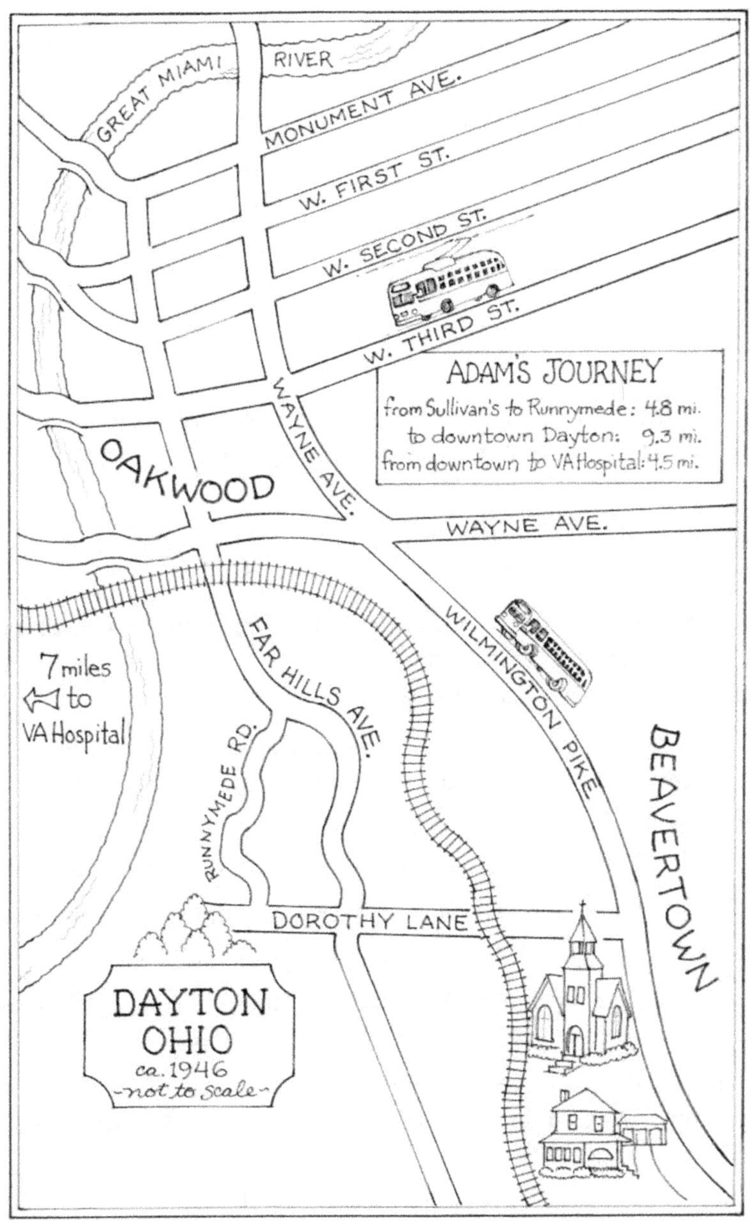
GREAT MIAMI RIVER
MONUMENT AVE.
W. FIRST ST.
W. SECOND ST.
W. THIRD ST.
WAYNE AVE.
OAKWOOD
ADAM'S JOURNEY
from Sullivan's to Runnymede: 4.8 mi.
to downtown Dayton: 9.3 mi.
from downtown to VA Hospital: 4.5 mi.
WAYNE AVE.
7 miles to VA Hospital
FAR HILLS AVE.
RUNNYMEDE RD.
WILMINGTON PIKE
BEAVERTOWN
DOROTHY LANE
DAYTON
OHIO
ca. 1946
-not to scale-

Acknowledge

Thank you to Vicki Borgman for reading and editing *Escape from the Shadows.* Your suggestions are helpful and creative. I value your keen eyes.

Thanks Bill Helm and Debi Lindhorst for your careful editing. The words I see are what I thought I wrote, not what is actually there.

A real thanks to Donna Brewer. You believed in and loved *Escape from the Belfry*. You couldn't wait for the sequel, *Escape from the Shadows.* Here it is—just for you.

A big thank you to my friend, Mary Coons. You took my ideas and turned them into a map I could never have drawn. You are so gifted!

Thanks to Debi Lindhorst of The Type Galley in Warren, Indiana for the wonderful cover. You see my vision and put it into a book cover.

Thank you to Bonnie Tobey Manning who took the great photo on the back cover. You are gifted. www.printroom.com/pro/btmanning.

I really appreciate my group of Reading Partners who agreed to read the manuscript and give me their opinion. Thank you.

As always, thanks to the wonderful writers group I belong to, Soli deo Gloria – to God be the Glory. You are all so encouraging, helpful and honest at the same time.

Table of Contents

Dedication

To all those with a superhero buried within them but didn't know it, until they tested their cape.

Prologue

Adam Schumacher's father, William, did not come home when WWII was over. Was Pops killed in action? Adam and his mother, Bridget, had not received notification. Was Pops a deserter?

Adam received a clue that Pops may be in a VA hospital, suffering from amnesia. Although Adam is only sixteen years old, he will leave his home in Indiana, go to Ohio and try to find him. What he finds, is far more dangerous than he ever imagined.

Chapter 1
Easter Break – 1946

Nearly a Year After the end of World War II in Europe

Adam slammed his locker door closed and hurried down the hall past Mr. Humphrey's classroom. "Bye, Mr. Humphrey," he said as he hurried passed his history teacher. "Have a nice Easter break."

Adam's anger and frustration were hard to hide beneath clenched teeth and taut shoulders, but he was always polite. All those months around last Christmas when he hid out in the belfry of the church on Cranberry Street, Shaddi, whom Adam first called the Wizard, stayed with him, comforting him and guiding him. Shaddi helped him discern the creepy guys who broke into the church and stole the precious Christ Child statue, from the good folks who helped him survive. Black shadows oozed up and belched their putrid stench when evil was around. By contrast, good people glowed with a light of love. It didn't help Adam's growing anger and impatience over his missing father that he saw the good glow around Humphrey's body. He was hard to dislike.

Mr. Humphrey had just lectured on the great loss in human life from the war. Adam was not ready to concede that Pops may have died on the battle field. Why did Shaddi have to complicate things? Adam thought Shaddi was just the spirit of the belfry. Now, he was showing up in strange places, even the paper-strewn halls of his high school at the end of the school day.

Pops had talked to him about Shaddi before he went off to the European theater of war. Adam didn't remember much of what Pops said but he knew that Shaddi would always be with him and would give him strength. Even when Moms was in the tuberculosis sanatorium, Shaddi had stayed with him as Adam snuck into the church tower to live. While no one else heard Shaddi or knew he was there, Adam felt his presence in the lonely cold belfry in the dark of the night, and didn't feel alone anymore.

"Adam, wait up," Frederica Breman called after her long-legged friend as he hurried toward the school's west exit. She flipped her sweater around her shoulders and scurried after him, careful not to run. It wouldn't have been proper for the science teacher and basketball coach's daughter to run in the school hallway. "I don't own stilts, Adam," she grumbled as she walked and skipped, trying to fall in step beside him. "My legs aren't as long as yours." Her blond ponytail bopped up and down on her back as she avoided a gallop.

"Fritzy, I..." Adam stammered without looking in her direction.

"I nothing, mister. It's me who can't keep up," she teased. "Slow down."

"May I see you before you go, Adam?" Mr. Humphrey interrupted as he motioned to Adam from his classroom door. His arms hung on each side of the doorjamb. He looked tired and ready for Easter break.

Adam slowed and turned around. "Uh, Mr. Humphrey, I'm in a bit of a hurry."

"I know you are, son," Humphrey drew out in his out-of-state southern accent. "It'll only take a minute." He turned and went back into his room evidently sure Adam would follow him.

Adam walked into the classroom he left just minutes before. Humphrey's lecture notes were still on the blackboard.

The Human Cost of World War II

USA	*407,300 military died*
United Kingdom	*383,700 military died – 67,200 civilians*
Germany	*4,440,000 to 5,318,000 military – 1,500,000 to 3,000,000 civilians*
Japan	*2,100,000 to 2,300,000 military – 550,000 to 800,000 civilians*
Jews	*Between 5,000,000 and 6,000,000 died in the Holocaust*

The Atom Bomb

August 6, 1945	*Hiroshima bombed*	*80,000 Japanese died*
August 9, 1945	*Nagasaki bombed*	*40,000 Japanese died*

"Adam," Mr. Humphrey pointed to the front desk in the center of the room. "Sit down a second, please."

"No thanks. I'll just stand." Adam shifted from one foot to the other and watched Fritzy waiting for him in the hall. He was glad to see her one more time before he left, although for the life of him he didn't know why. He saw Fritzy every day and had since he wore a Cub Scout uniform.

"I know today's lecture upset you," Humphrey began.

"I'm fine," Adam denied, then turned and pointed to the blackboard. With measured words, he explained, "My father is not one of those." He gestured toward the top statistic of U.S. military killed in the war. His voice was coarse and insistent.

"I never said he was," Mr. Humphrey said softly and put his hand on Adam's shoulder.

Adam moved a little releasing his teacher's hand on him. "I gotta go," he mumbled softly but his words were sure.

Humphry started to reach out again but withdrew his hand. "In fact, Adam, I really wanted you to know, I believe in what you're doing."

Adam's eyes flashed back to Humphrey. "You believe me?" Smiling a little, his spine uncoiled as his height grew back to its full stature.

"You said that a Sergeant told you he had seen a man he believed to be your father and he gave you your dad's dog tags," Humphrey said as he picked up the eraser and haphazardly began to wipe off the blackboard. Then he turned back to Adam and added quietly, "I couldn't go into the military. As the whole class knows, I'm deaf in my right ear and blind in my right eye. Dynamite explosions, opening the coal mines I worked in while in college, blew them out." He put the eraser on the chalk tray. Pulling a money clip from his pocket, he peeled off a ten-dollar bill. "Here, Adam. I want to help pay for your trip to search for your dad. Gas is twenty-one cents a gallon you know."

"Mr. Humphrey," Adam began as he held up both hands with palms out. "I couldn't. I have to do this myself. Besides, holy cow, that's almost a fourth of your weekly pay check."

"How would you know how much money I make?" Humphrey challenged him teasingly.

Adam fixed his eyes on his shoes. "Fritzy's dad and I talked about possible jobs after college and how much money I could make." He cleared his throat and added, "I hope I didn't offend you."

"No, not at all. They publish teacher's salaries in the newspaper every year. It's the amount that's offensive." He chuckled as he patted Adam on the shoulder. "Please," Humphrey protested as he folded the money and stuffed it into Adam's shirt pocket. Then, his eyes grew misty. "I couldn't help our boys in Europe or the Pacific. Please, it would be my honor to help you find your father, Adam."

Adam stared at the colorful flecks in the otherwise dark linoleum on the floor. Finally, he said, "Thank you, Mr. Humphrey." He offered his hand. "I know I can do it," he said and then turned and left the room, wiping his eyes on his shirt sleeve.

As he came out of the classroom Adam took a big red handkerchief from his hip pocket and blew his nose. With his face nearly covered with the hanky and his eyes closed, he forgot all about Frederica who was still waiting near the water fountain. He aimed his face again toward the side door.

"Adam, wait," Fritzy called as she ran to catch up with Adam Schumacher's long strides. They got to the side door at the same time and pushed their way out into the sunlight.

Once out on the sidewalk, a ruby throated hummingbird fluttered above, then landed on Adam's shoulder. "Can you imagine a hummingbird already, this early in the spring?" Fritzy gasped. "And, one tame enough to perch on a human."

Adam spoke slowly and softly as he reached out his index finger for the little flitter to jump on. "Rudy was here all winter. If I hadn't had the little hummingbird with me in the belfry, I would have been completely alone."

"Do you think this one is Rudy?" Fritzy stared at the hummer as it jumped up on Adam's extended finger.

Adam smiled at the little bird. "Rudy lived with me all winter in that cold belfry. You know, with Moms and Pops both gone, I was all alone out there on the farm. And then, the coal for the furnace ran out." He smiled at the hummer and moved his finger around to see the little bird from every angle. "I had to let Rudy go in late winter. Mr. and Mrs. Gunderman offered the little apartment Mrs. Gunderman's mother lived in at the back of the house when Moms got out of the hospital. It wasn't fair for Moms and me to finally have a great little cottage to live in while Rudy was caged up in the belfry." Adam watched the hummer as its wings fanned into a blur and it lifted off and flew into the trees beyond the school. He kept his eyes on the little bird until he couldn't see the hummer any more. "If I really thought that little guy was my hummingbird, I don't think I could leave on break."

Fritzy bounced along. "Speaking of leaving, why are you in such a hurry? You're not starting out until tomorrow." Fritzy skipped a little to stay up. "Slow down, will ya?" She tried to grab hold of his shirt sleeve but missed.

"Can't," he insisted and kept going. "And, yeah, tomorrow was my first plan," Adam admitted as he pulled his ball cap down to keep it from blowing away in the spring breeze. He smiled. "This is a great Indiana April. Easter is late this year, the twenty-first. I've been checking the Farmer's Almanac for when the neighboring farmer will plant our fields. That's Moms only income. Since Pops isn't here, it's my job to look out for her interests. With Easter being late, the weather will be fantastic for traveling—balmy, in the mid-sixties."

"This last winter was hard," Fritzy agreed. "It seemed like the snow would never stop." She paused and then added, "Wait a moment, Adam, you said 'first plan.' Are you changing your mind? You said you lost that guy's address. How will you know where to look for your dad? Will you still be here on Palm Sunday?" Questions spilled from Fritzy Breman's lips like she had dropped an open box of marbles. "Will you be back when school starts after break—back for the Spring Fling?"

"I'm not sure," Adam paused and then wanted to move on. "Wait, I have to be back for school."

"Well, if you're here..." Two obnoxious boys pushed past Fritzy and shoved their way along the sidewalk that led from the Middletown High School building to the string of bright yellow school buses.

"Hey, watch out," she protested. They trampled her freshly polished saddle shoes and splattered dirt up on her white bobby socks. "Well, of all the nerve!" She shouted after them with her hands firmly planted on her hips. "They may be in the same class we're in," she yelled as her voice raised, "but they're not from our species."

Adam started to holler at them until he heard them continue to argue between themselves. "They are their own worst enemy," he said as he shook his head in disgust. He watched as black shadows oozed out of the concrete of the walkway and wrapped their ugly tentacles around the boys' legs. Adam could hear the idiot boys' stupid conversation.

"Buddy, I said—'Quit pushing me around.' So...stop it!" Freddy Alexander shoved back as the two bounced off each other on the sidewalk. Buddy stumbled off the concrete and stepped in a pile of dog poo. Adam could see a dark shadow push back.

Adam and Fritzy laughed quietly. They didn't want trouble, but it was hard not to find two such clowns sadly amusing.

"Freddy, yuck, you made a mess!" Buddy gasped. As he stepped back on the walk, he wiped the soles and sides of his shoes on the grass beside the path. "I should make you clean this stuff up."

"Try an' make me," Freddy laughed as they brushed passed some of the other kids without so much as an, "Excuse me." Once they were in the parking lot, they disappeared among the old jalopies and war surplus jeeps.

"What are those two up to this time?" Adam shook his head as he watched the boys act like fools. He knew them, although he was glad he didn't know them well. But, he did know their secret. In his mind, he remembered hiding in the shadows of the Cranberry Street Church when the two broke in and stole the valuable Christ Child carving. Adam was also the one who had stolen it back and returned it to the church before Christmas. The two thieves didn't get into trouble because no one else knew about it.

Adam watched the two roughnecks for a moment in disbelief. "How can anyone—" Then, he dropped the useless pair from his thoughts and quickly added, "Sorry, Fritzy, I gotta run. I'll talk to you later." With that, he hurried toward the parking lot where Pops' big 1937 Diamond T truck waited.

"Adam," Fritzy called. "But—," she whispered after him, "the Spring Fling?" Fritzy stood in the middle of the walk and shielded her eyes from the bright sun. "Call me," she shouted. "Or...I'll call you."

"Okay, gotta get gas," he hollered back, opened the red truck door, stepped up onto the running board and jumped in. He smiled as he ran his fingers over the steering wheel and inhaled the memory of his family's farm. Since his grandparents' deaths, Pops' absence and Moms' long illness, the house key in his pocket and the key to the truck were the only links he had to his home. His recent birthday made him finally old enough to drive the heavy truck on the streets. He felt the thickness of his billfold in his hip pocket, pulled it out and placed it on the seat beside him. Adam had saved money for the trip from his work as assistant janitor at his church. Now, he was ready to find the man with the answers.

Last December, a stranger in a blue car left a clue to Pops' whereabouts with Pastor Silverman. Pastor said the man's name was Sergeant Smith. Now that Easter break was here, Adam was ready to find the Sergeant, and perhaps even his father. The minister had given him a small piece of paper with the Sergeant's address and phone number on it. But, Adam had lost it before he had been able to write the first letter.

The man seemed to be all over Middletown in his blue car. Adam had been afraid because he believed the man was stalking him. He feared the man might be a representative of the Child Welfare League, those who cared for war orphans and other abandoned kids. Goodness knows Adam felt abandoned, living alone on the farm and then, hiding in the cold drafty church belfry. Adam was afraid to let the man get close enough to him to explain himself. Before the Sergeant left, the blue-car man talked to Pastor Silverman and Pastor had told Adam of the conversation.

Silverman repeated the words to Adam exactly as he remembered. "I'm Sergeant Smith, Pastor. I have been looking for the Schumacher family. There is a boy around town who I think might know the family, but for some reason, he won't speak to me. I have been away from my family for a long time. I have to get back." Then, the part that rang in Adam's ears, gave him new hope.

"I work in a Veteran's Administration Hospital in Dayton, Ohio," the Sergeant had said. "I talked to a veteran there who said he had seen a man in one of the VA's who was injured and unable to remember his own name. He was sure it was William Schumacher. I need to let his family know and give them the dog tags that were found near where Schumacher had been taken prisoner of war at the Battle of the Bulge."

Adam had two clues: a VA hospital and Pops' dog tags the Sergeant had left with Pastor Silverman. He was determined to find that same Sergeant Smith and get more clues to his father's location. Adam was sure he could bring Pops home. Long before the Sergeant showed up, Adam had feared that Pops hadn't come home because he didn't want to. It may be possible that Pops had amnesia and therefore didn't know where home was. He had to find him. He had to.

Chapter 2
Up to No Good

"Why did we come here anyway?" Freddy slouched down in Buddy's car and peeked over the dashboard as Buddy pulled into Alfred Gunderman's driveway. "I see that Shoemaker kid at school every day and even on Sundays at church when Mom and Dad make me go. Why do we have to show up here?" He pulled his dirty Cubs ball cap down as far as he could and peered at the house from under the brim. His dad had brought the cap home from someplace and Freddy wore it all the time.

Buddy sneered. "Like I already told you, Freddy, we gotta get even with that guy. Ol' Shoemaker thinks he's better and smarter than us." Buddy lowered his voice as he opened the car door and got out. Both doors squeaked on their rusty hinges so the boys carefully closed the doors without latching them in order to keep the noise level down. Dark shadows writhed and contorted their ugly dance as they followed Buddy and Freddy out of the car. Unaware of their presence, the boys moved as quietly as they could, up onto Gunderman's front porch.

"Let's go, Buddy," Freddy pleaded. His shoulders slumped, forcing his back into a miserable S-shape. "I don't like this. Shoemaker did us a favor. He kept us out of jail. No one but him knows it was us." He brushed back his unruly hair by adjusting his hat and covered his mouth with his hand.

Buddy Phillips pushed the doorbell. "Yeah and all we have to do is look at him the wrong way and he can call the cops," he spoke through gritted teeth. "He even gave us the name of the policeman—Overton—so we can turn ourselves in, if we want to, and stop the anxiety."

"We already have the precious note he needs to find his dad," Freddy said. "Some Sergeant signed it. Shoemaker dropped it at church. You already know we picked it up. Without the note, he has no trail to follow. Isn't that enough?" He whispered as the sound of people stirring came from inside the house.

"Not for me," Buddy grumbled. "That sure isn't enough for me."

"Hi, boys," Arletta Gunderman smiled when she opened the door. "I recognize you two from the cafeteria line at school."

"Yes, Ma'am," Buddy oozed sticky politeness. "You're one of our school cafeteria ladies."

"Right," Freddy grinned, "but school's out now."

"No one is happier that Easter break is here than I am," Mrs. Gunderman chuckled. "What can I do for you two?" She wiped her hands on a spare tea towel she had brought from the kitchen. The aroma of fried chicken, in the browning, simmer stage, drifted out on her apron.

"We wondered if Mr. Gunderman is home," Buddy smiled with a silly grin. "We'd like to talk to him."

Mrs. G. looked down at Buddy's shoes. The odor was nasty in the open breeze of the front porch. If he wore them in the house, the odor could be strong enough to spoil any appetite for supper. "You two leave your shoes there on the porch, beside the door. Then, you'll find Mr. Gunderman in his chair in front of the living room window."

Buddy untied his shoe laces carefully. As careless as he had been when he stepped into the doggy-doo, it appeared he didn't want any of the dog-muffins on his hands or other clothing.

Mrs. G. opened the door wide and stepped out of the way. "Come on in."

The two roughnecks had no trouble slithering around in the middle of the night to steal a sacred carving from the church where Mr. Gunderman was the janitor. Now, they slowly shuffled farther into the house, their heads nearly touching their chests, like scolded puppies. They knew they were guilty of a major art theft, and their posture and countenance showed it, even if the Gundermans were unaware of their past deed.

"Well hello you two balcony sitters," Alfred Gunderman said as he smiled and watched the boys with a suspicious eye.

"Yeah, we sit up there on Sunday mornings, when we're there," Freddy admitted.

"So, what brings you here?" Mr. G. asked.

"Well, ah..." Buddy stumbled over his words and shuffled back and forth as he struggled to answer.

"Sit down boys. Take your hats off and make yourselves comfortable," Alfred offered as he pointed to the sofa.

"Thanks," Freddy slipped onto the sofa in a heap, nearly coming to rest on his neck.

"Shoemaker is a friend of ours," Buddy began as his grin took a weak twist and seemed to slip off his face. "We know that he works for you at the church, sweeping and stuff." He looked over at Freddy slumped on the couch.

"He does," Mr. G. agreed. "Adam is a good worker." Then he added, "You know he changed his name back to Schumacher since the war is over. Many still have hard feelings over German sounding names, don't ya know—even though his family came to America more than a hundred and fifty years ago."

"Well, we hear he's goin' on a little trip over Easter break," Buddy hedged. "Where's he goin'?"

Gunderman lowered his head and looked intently past hooded eyebrows at the two boys. "Oh, I don't think that's my story to tell," he said slowly. "You'll have to ask him—he bein' a friend of yours and all."

"Yes, sir, I suppose you're right," Buddy spoke as he thought about how to get the answers he needed.

"No s'pose to it." Mr. Gunderman eyed the boys narrowly. "Is that why you came by here?" He leaned toward the pair of misfits.

"No, we were just curious about his fancy vacation. You know, the ocean side or mountain cabin," Buddy feigned enthusiasm. "What we really wanted to know was...ah...if we could volunteer to do some of Shoemaker's, ah Schumacher's, work while he's gone."

Alfred's eyes narrowed to fine slits, "Well now that's mighty generous of you." He checked the two up and down.

Freddy was practically lying down on the couch beside Buddy. The holes in his socks revealed toenails badly in need of trimming.

Buddy was biting his fingernails and tapping the heels of his feet up and down in rapid tempo. "We just want to help. When is he leaving?"

"Well now, you sure want to know a lot about that young man's business." The old man spoke slowly. "Why haven't you asked him? Are you sure he's a friend of yours?"

Buddy ran his fingers through his hair. "I guess you're right. He's not in our classes, so we don't always run into him at school."

As Alfred watched them, a small smile crossed his face. "He's not back from school yet, but as to the church work, Adam will have it all done before he leaves—sorry. He's been workin' real hard, don't ya know."

Buddy fidgeted, and Freddy lay like a slug for a moment longer. Finally, Buddy stood up and pulled on Freddy's sleeve. "Come on. We'd better go."

"You're just in time," Mr. Gunderman said and watched the boys' reactions. "That looks like Adam's truck down the block there a piece."

"Great. Let's beat it, Freddy," Buddy said. The boys sprinted for the front door, darted out, slipped on their shoes without tying them, stumbled to the driveway and hopped into Buddy's old sedan his father gave him. They pulled out of the driveway as Adam came within three houses of the Gunderman home.

• • •

Adam stared at the worn out jalopy as the boys sped off in the opposite direction. He pulled to the curb in front of the house and parked. He couldn't take his eyes off the beat up old wreck rattling down the street as he walked to the door.

"Hello?" he hollered as he entered the house. Adam and his mother had become very friendly with Arletta and Alfred. After Adam's hard work as Alfred's assistant at the

Church, the two families forged a bond. That friendship provided a temporary apartment in the guest cottage behind the Gunderman home for Adam and his mother. But, he was still polite about just barging in their front door.

"Come on in, my boy," Alfred called without moving from his chair in front of the window, his observation post on the front-line of life.

"What did those two guys want?" Adam asked as he walked to the window and careened his head to see the two thieves drive away. No one else knew that the pair was more than a nuisance. The two of them were in league with the dark shadows, the evil ones his granny had warned him about. Adam had seen the black ones ooze out of hiding when the boys were around. The stench of the dark ones made him gag.

Gunderman clasped his hands in front of him as if he had come to a conclusion about Freddy and Buddy. "They wanted to know when you were leaving on your trip. They said they wanted your job at the church while you're gone." Alfred chuckled as he settled back in his chair. "Can you imagine those two working for an hour—anywhere? At anything?"

"No, I can't," Adam mumbled as he turned and faced Alfred—his friend, landlord and boss. "Did you tell them when I'm going to leave to go find Pops?"

"That wasn't for me to say," Alfred stated flatly.

"Thank you, Mr. G. Moms and I have been talking about it. Today was the last day of school before the break. If I leave early tomorrow morning, I can be into Ohio, settle in and then check the VA hospital on Sunday morning. They might have longer visiting hours on the weekend."

Gunderman's face brightened with hope. "You can maybe get a lead on Sergeant Blue-Car-Man from the Veteran's Administration. Besides, you have his address. If your dad isn't at the Dayton VA, they might be able to direct you on into Pennsylvania. There are many VA hospitals."

"Blue-Car-Man is Sergeant Smith. The card he left with Pastor Silverman said Smith is an employee at the VA," Adam said. "Maybe even a doctor. There were the initials, M.D., after his name."

"And...Easter Sunday?" Mr. G asked. "Will you be back for the holiest Sunday of the year?"

"I'll find a church for Palm Sunday, somewhere, but I hope to be back here by Easter," Adam said slowly as he watched Buddy's car cruise by the house again. "What do those two want?"

"Why don't you leave after the services on Sunday or even Monday morning?" Alfred suggested. "Your mother has been feeling strong enough to attend church. Palm Sunday would be a time for the two of you to go together."

"That's true," Adam closed his eyes as he tried to rethink his plan. "And, I'd be there to roll the heavy wooden dividing sanctuary door up for you. Your heart is doing better, but you're not ready for that."

"Now, see here, son. This isn't about me," Mr. G. protested.

"I'm sorry, no. I'm not saying that—I just mean—I could do that for you." Adam dusted off his pants and sat down on the sofa facing the window.

"Any number of twelve or thirteen-year-old boys would be happy to roll it up." The old man watched Adam who continued to survey the street. "Fritzy called. She asked too when you're leaving. You should have placed an announcement in the *Middletown Gazette*. She wanted to ask you and your mom to come for Sunday dinner."

"Okay," Adam answered as he continued his surveillance of the street out front.

"What is all this patrolling and trolling about? Those two upstarts have driven by this house three times now," Mr. G. asked as he watched them pass again. "I wouldn't have asked, but you seem overly interested in them."

"I have no idea what they want, but I know they can't be trusted. Please, will you keep an eye on Moms while I'm gone?" Adam asked.

"You know we will," Alfred agreed. Then he added, "If you leave tomorrow morning, or even Sunday, you'll have to stay over. The full VA staff won't be back on duty until Monday morning. Where will you stay? Do you have money for a hotel room? A store-bought room can be really expensive."

"There's gotta be some belfry I can sleep in," Adam smiled as he thought of the three months he hid at night in the dark belfry of the church pastored by Reverend Silverman. "And, the weather is warmer now for a campout like that."

"Now, we'll have none of that kind of talk," Mr. G. cautioned. "Mrs. Gunderman's niece and her family live in Beavertown, just south of Dayton. I know you can sleep on the couch there for a night or two. You could attend Palm Sunday services with them. Then, Monday morning, you'll be ready to talk to the right people at the VA."

"Mr. Gunderman, Pops and Gramps taught me never to be beholdin' to outsiders." Adam shook his head.

"I said she's a niece, Adam, not a stranger," Alfred challenged him. "Besides, I don't think being beholdin' is your concern this time. I think meeting people you don't know is more your problem."

"I don't know—."

"Well, I do," Alfred settled the matter. "They rent out their upstairs to roomers. The Sullivan family sleeps on studio couches in various rooms on the main floor, even have a bed set up in the dinette for the wife and her husband. They are used to having others in the house. You won't bother them at all." Alfred reached for a small piece of paper from the side table next to his chair. "Here ya go," he began as he handed Adam the note. "The missus wrote it all out. Mr. and Mrs. Daniel Sullivan, Grace is the niece, 1524 Keystone Avenue, Dayton, Ohio. Their phone number is there, too. Mrs. Gunderman will call her this evening. Grace will be expecting you. Now stuff that paper down in your pocket so you don't forget it."

"I guess I can do that," Adam agreed. "I just don't want to be a bother." Adam stood at the window another minute.

"Thanks. But—I still think I'll leave tomorrow morning. I have waited so long for Pops to come home, I can't wait any longer."

"I know," Alfred said. "It's hard when a dad is gone. When you don't know where he is or if and when he'll be home, that makes it even harder. You can wait a long time if you know how much time you have to spend waitin'."

"I never told you before…," Adam paused and wondered if he should even tell anyone his deepest fears. "I even thought Pops was a defector. I had a whole story worked out. I decided that was why he didn't come home after the war was over—why we hadn't heard from him in over a year, even after the other dads came home."

"I'm so sorry I didn't know that. We could have talked about it," Gunderman assured him.

"There's no way you could have known. I didn't tell anyone." Adam fixed his eyes on the outside. "The answers are out there some place. I'm itching to find them. I have no brothers or sister. I'm the only one who can get to the bottom of this. If I can find out what happened to Pops, I'll be able to find him." He looked again toward the street but he wasn't looking for the two ne'er-do-wells. He was plotting a plan to find his father, William Schumacher.

He already knew the facts: between December 16, 1944 and January 25, 1945, the German forces drove deeper into the Ardennes, a densely forested region of Wallonia in Belgium, France and Luxembourg on the Western Front, to secure bridges. The U.S. and Allies began to turn around to protect the troops and caused the Allied line to look like a bulge. From that point on, it was known as the Battle of the Bulge. The United States military suffered over 100,000 casualties, but Adam refused to believe Pops was one of them. Almost worse, maybe Pops didn't come home because of something Adam did. Then there was the picture in the news magazine of those taken as POW's during the Battle of the Bulge. One looked a lot like Pops. Sergeant Smith gave Adam Pops' dog tags, found on the battle field. Adam was determined to find out what really happened.

Chapter 3
The Decision Is Made

"Adam, it's for you." Bridget Schumacher smiled as she handed her son the telephone. "It's Fritzy."

"Oh no, I didn't call her back," he moaned as he took the receiver. "Hi, Fritzy."

"You didn't call me," she said, sounding disappointed. "I hope it's not too late. I don't know what time your mother goes to bed. I know she needs her rest," she apologized.

"It's okay. We're still up." Adam shuffled the receiver to the other ear. "It's not your fault. I should have phoned you."

"I called because I wondered if you've decided when you're going to leave." Her voice sounded funny to Adam.

Why does she sound like she's holding her breath? He thought it but absolutely did not say it out loud. "I talked to Moms," he told her. "I'm going to load up about 7AM tomorrow and head out then. That way, maybe I'll be home for Easter Sunday morning. I'll stay at the Sullivans' home tomorrow evening and then go out to the VA on Sunday morning. Maybe I can get a lead on Pops from other patients or their visitors."

"Who are the Sullivans?" Fritzy asked.

"Mrs. Sullivan is Arletta Gunderman's niece," Adam answered as he watched out the front window for the two good-for-nothings who kept driving past. "The Sullivans live south of Dayton."

"Oh, okay." She was quiet for a minute.

Adam didn't like to talk on the phone most of time. And, he sure didn't like awkward, icky silence. "Fritz, are you there?"

"Yup, I'm here." Fritzy still didn't sound like herself. "It's just that," she paused and started again, faster than before. "I would have invited you and your mom to come for Sunday dinner. This way, if you're back in time, maybe all three of you can come over for Easter Sunday, your father, too."

With his head down, Adam studied the flooring under his feet. "That would be great Fritzy." He was silent a minute more. "If I'm not back, maybe Moms can join you all on Easter."

"Well, first of all, you have to be back because you'll need to rest up for school on Monday. And, I'd like to invite your mother for dinner this Sunday, too. Do you want me to talk to her?"

"No, that's okay. Hold on..." He placed the receiver on his shoulder. "Moms, Fritzy is inviting you for Sunday dinner on Palm Sunday."

"That's very nice, Adam, but...does Fritzy's mother know she has extended the invitation? I wouldn't want to impose." Bridget Schumacher was not one to horn in; Adam knew that.

He chuckled to himself, "Where have I heard that before? Just a minute." Again, he spoke into the telephone. "Is it all right with your mom?"

"Mother is the one who suggested that I ask her," Fritzy insisted.

"It's good, Moms," Adam reassured her. "Mrs. Breman invited you."

"Tell Fritzy thank you. I'll be there," Bridget said and smiled.

"She'll be there. Wish I could come, too." He blushed, but he knew Fritzy couldn't see the heat in his cheeks.

"Me, too," Fritzy agreed. "Well, bye. I'll talk to you when you get back."

Adam hung up and smiled. Things had changed so much in the last eight months. First, he was alone in the church's belfry while Moms was in the hospital, and now he and Moms lived in Gundermans' warm, modern cottage behind their home. Now, it seemed that things were changing between him and Fritzy.

"I'm going on to bed, Honey," Bridget announced. "You should, too. You have a big day tomorrow." His mother went into the bedroom and closed the door.

Adam headed for the window seat and took the bedding from the storage cubby beneath the cushion. He flipped the sheet open, tucked it under the couch cushions and spread a blanket over the top. As he settled down for the night, he could see through the window that the sky was beginning to lose the star shine. Low hanging spring clouds were dropping a mist on the ground and darkness began to take command of his world.

That night, even though the sofa was comfortable, Adam tossed a little before he found his comfortable spot. "Shaddi," he whispered into the night, "you were with me in the belfry, be with Moms while I'm gone. And, check in on me too as I travel. Spirit of the belfry, I am amazed. You are everywhere. Be with Pops too, wherever he is." In minutes, Adam was asleep.

• • •

It was two A.M. Out in the street, in front of the house, there was a little pop, like the sound of a BB gun, and then the street light shattered and went out. In the darkness, two figures moved quickly down the sidewalk, a block from where they had left their car, and stowed their pop gun. There could be no noise near the house.

"Got the gas can, Freddy?" Buddy stopped by the curb in front of the Gunderman house where Adam had parked his truck.

"Of course. Do you have the rubber hose?" Freddy mocked with a smirk.

"That's why we came, Freddy Boy. That's why we came," Buddy whispered.

The truck's gas cap unscrewed easily. Buddy placed it silently on the sidewalk where he could easily find it again in the dark.

"Are you sure you got the right truck? Gunderman has a truck too ya know," Freddy announced sarcastically.

"Freddy, Gunderman parks his truck in the garage. Besides, haven't you seen Shoemaker all over the school parking lot behind that V-shaped radiator up front with the flashy chrome grill? I'm sick of seeing him."

The two unrepentant thieves worked quickly. Buddy, the ring-leader, shoved the end of a small diameter hose into the gas tank, sucked out some of the air, then pinched off the end until he placed it into the opening of a large, five gallon can he had brought with him. With the can placed lower than the truck gas tank, he slowly siphoned off the top five gallons of gasoline Adam had just put in the truck after school.

"Okay, wise guy," Buddy snickered, "you're going to get about seventy miles less than you thought you were." He removed the hose, drained the remaining gas from the tube into the street, coiled it up and looped a length of twine around it.

"Right," Freddy giggled. "Maybe he'll be out in the middle of nowhere when the engine sputters and stops."

"We can only be so lucky," Buddy stifled a laugh as he replaced the gas cap. "Too bad we won't be there to see it."

"Maybe we will," Freddy stated as his face lit up with a new idea.

In their usual modus operandi, they slithered around in the dark of night, and left their havoc behind. This time, they wouldn't even see the fruits of their devious labor. But then, darkness needs no light to make its presence known.

Chapter 4
An Early Start

The sun sent shimmering light beams across the empty sofa of the little cottage. Adam was up. He had folded his bedding and had stashed it all in the window seat. When his mother came into the kitchen, he was sitting at the table eating a bowl of corn flakes.

"I hope I didn't wake you up," he apologized.

"What do you mean you didn't want to wake me up?" Bridget playfully smacked Adam on the shoulder. "You're not leaving here without a proper send off."

"You need your rest," Adam cautioned.

"Don't you worry about me. I can nap all day if I want to." Moms poured a cup of coffee and sat down with him while he ate. The back yard, colored and growing in the light green shades of spring, stretched out beyond the cottage window. Bridget smiled.

"Looks like the grass will be ready to mow by the time I get home," Adam thought out loud. From the window view, Adam wondered if anything could be more perfect. He had a fat billfold, a full tank of gas, and a small war surplus duffel bag stuffed with several changes of clothes.

"You bring your daddy back with you and he can help rake and trim while you mow." His mother sipped her coffee and blew across the rim of the cup. "You make a good cup of joe."

"Thank you," he smiled and checked his watch "I'd better be going."

"I know," she whispered. "I'll walk out to the truck with you."

"No, Moms, please. One of the things the doctor told you when he released you from the sanitarium was, don't catch a cold. The air might be damp out there if the dew is still on the ground. It isn't summer yet."

"Well, alright. I don't really want you to go, so, if I can't see you leave, maybe I won't worry as much. Besides, if I stay in, that will be my chance to drink another cup of coffee before I go back to bed."

"Will you be able to sleep after two cups of coffee?"

"Have you forgotten how much I have been sleeping since I got home?" Bridget placed her hands on the table and raised herself from the chair. She threw her arms open for a big hug. It would be the last she would see Adam for many days.

"Bye Moms. I'll call you from wherever I get at the end of the day. My plan is to stay tonight at Mrs. Gunderman's niece's home—Grace Sullivan—in Beavertown, Ohio." Adam gave his mother another hug, grabbed up his duffle and went out the front door.

He walked along the sidewalk to the right of the house and out to the street. The large canvas he had borrowed from Mr. G. made a good camouflage for items beneath and out of sight. He started to stash his bag under a corner of the protective cover, hoping it would discourage anyone from snatching the bag out of the back. If they didn't see it, it might be safe. Changing his mind, he stowed the duffle bag on the seat up front.

"Wait, Adam," Mrs. Gunderman called from the house. She hurried along the front walk with a brown paper sack in her hand and pulled her sweater around her arms against the cool morning air. "Now, this is two peanut butter and strawberry jam sandwiches and a dozen chocolate chip cookies. I know you like that kind. They came out of the oven just a little while ago."

"Mrs. G., you didn't have to do that," Adam smiled sheepishly.

"Of course I didn't have to, Adam. I wanted to, so here you are." She handed over the treasure in the paper bag and wiped her hands on her apron. With both of her hands placed on his shoulders, she looked him straight in the eyes.

"Adam, you have become like a grandson to Alfred and me. I don't know what I would have done without you and your mother here to keep an eye on that old scamp of a husband of mine after his second heart attack. We love you, and we will be praying for your safety." She gave him a hug and added, "Now, it's our turn. We'll keep our eye on your mother so's you won't have to worry."

"Thanks, Mrs. G. You and Mr. G. have been great." Adam gave her a hug, then turned and put the lunch sack on the truck seat. With one foot on the running board and a hand on the steering wheel, he hopped up into the cab, started the engine, put it in gear and slowly pulled away from the curb.

Adam was on his way. The gas tank was full, even if he had no gauge to monitor it. He would calculate the miles he had driven by the distance between towns and divide that by the number of miles he got per gallon. It was rough, but he shouldn't run out of gas. With Shaddi at his side, he would find

Pops and bring him home. Adam wouldn't have to hang his head in shame any more. He had already faced his name. Whether Schumacher or Shoemaker, he knew who he was and God did, too. Nothing more needed saying.

• • •

Adam made one stop. He opened the door of the church, entered and inhaled the memory of sugar cookies from the hospitality table and the sound of laughter from happy church friends who bubbled through the halls. The pastor's tabby cat, Gertrude, tiptoed over and draped her body around and through his legs.

"You'd better stay down here," Adam whispered to the cat as he quietly slipped up the ladder attached to the wall near the west entrance of the church. "The bell-tower room is no place for you." Even in the morning light, the stark room was colder and darker than he remembered.

"Shaddi?" He whispered into the shadows of the church's belfry. "I stopped in to say, goodbye. I can't stay long. I have to be on the road and not waste any daylight."

The morning sun burst from behind grey clouds, shimmered on the clear spring air and danced into the space far above the church's entry. There was no sound at first, only the desperate silence and the memory of the loneliness Adam had experienced all the many months he lived in the icy, dim space. Now, things were working out. Maybe, just maybe the Spirit would go with him.

Finally, his shoulders drooped with disappointment. "Shaddi, you were all that kept me going while Moms was in the hospital and Pops was M.I.A. Moms came home, but Pops didn't." Still, the spirit was silent.

"You were the only one who didn't ridicule me because my name was Schumacher," he coaxed out the spirit's presence. "When I started calling myself Shoemaker—that helped. It was safer that way, during the big war. The German sounding name was definitely not a positive thing during those years."

Adam shrugged and edged his way toward the trap door and the ladder that led below. A rustle of last autumn's leaves in the darkened corner drew his attention back into the space. "Shaddi?" he whispered. "Is that you?" But, there was only silence where once there had been comfort and companionship. Adam would have to leave without a goodbye.

Chapter 5
The Stowaway

Adam had left Indiana miles back and enjoyed the rolling hills of southern Ohio. Warm breezes blew in through the truck's open windows. "This is perfect," he whispered.

The growling from his stomach reminded him of the sack Mrs. Gunderman had sent with him. He kept his eyes on the road and fished in the bag for a couple of cookies. "Wow, there are tons of chocolate chips in these," he said and smiled.

The sun danced in and out of the cluster of trees along the side of the road. It felt like someone was taking hundreds of flash pictures as he passed. It began to bother his eyes, so he tried to pull the bill of his cap down and over to the side toward the light. "I need sunglasses," he talked out loud to the empty cab. "I have a little extra money with what Mr. Humphrey gave me. I'll get some."

The eastern route of the Dixie Highway through southern Ohio had service stations all along the way. When he was still north of Dayton, he couldn't take the bursts of light any longer and stopped at a SOHIO filling station.

"What can I do for you?" an attendant asked as he walked out of the service bay and onto the drive.

"I think I'll top off the gas tank. I shouldn't need much but I see your price is nineteen cents a gallon, which is two cents less than I paid yesterday in Indiana." Adam started for the station office, then turned, "Do you have sunglasses inside?"

"Sure, there on the wall beside the cash register. I'll be right there."

Inside the office, dotted liberally with oil smudges, there was an abundance of products on display: a counter case full of candy bars and newspapers separated the customers from the cash box. A Coca Cola cooler was off to the left, and the sunglasses the station attendant told him about hung from a display on the wall. He chose a pair of aviator glasses, tried them on and checked out how they looked in the small mirror attached to the display. As he studied their fit in the reflective glass, something from the station's drive caught his eye. Someone lifted the canvas from the bed of his truck, climbed out, and darted toward the side of the building where the restrooms were located.

Adam placed the glasses on the counter and started outside. "I'll be right back. I want those glasses, a candy bar and a coke. I'll pay for it all with the gas bill."

"Sure, take your time," the attendant agreed.

The building was white painted cinder block. The outside looked cleaner than the inside, so Adam leaned against the wall. In a moment, the door to the Ladies Room opened. Adam smiled, "Why, it's Miss Breman I believe."

Fritzy jumped, obviously rattled, and grabbed the door knob. "Adam Schumacher, you scared me to death."

"How do you think I feel? Everybody at home will probably think I kidnapped you!" He was half sputtering with anger and half stifling a giggle.

"Oh, I didn't think about that. Did you see a pay phone in there?" Fritzy sheepishly hurried toward the office.

"You didn't think about it?" Adam shook his head. He muttered to himself, "How is that possible?"

"Is everything alright," the station attendant questioned when he saw Fritzy come in. "I almost called the sheriff when I saw you climb out of that truck bed, Miss."

"Oh, sorry. I'm a friend of Adam's. I'm going with him on his Easter break trip."

"You are?" Adam and the attendant blurted out at the same time.

"I am," she stated flatly and dialed the operator. "Mister," she said as she dialed zero, "I'm going to make a long distance call but I'll reverse the charges."

"The boss isn't here but, that's okay." He leaned over and rearranged the candy bars and didn't get far from the phone.

"I'll take two Baby Ruth bars. Here's ten cents...and I'll take two bottles of pop from the cooler," Adam smiled and nodded in Fritzy's direction.

"I can pay for my own. I brought money, too," she insisted, then turned her attention to the telephone call. "Hello?" she said into the receiver. "I want to call Lincoln 3472 in Middletown, Indiana. And, please, reverse the charges."

Adam checked the clock on the wall. It was 12:30 P.M. No wonder he was hungry. He selected two bottles of coke from the icy water in the Coke chest. "How much do I owe you?" he asked the man.

"Five cents each for the two candy bars and another ten cents for the two cokes, that's twenty cents plus the fifteen gallons of gasoline for a dollar ninety, makes two dollars and a dime," he summed up the whole bill after putting all the data in the cash register.

"Fifteen gallons of gas? I just filled up yesterday. I must be getting terrible mileage. I'll have to have it looked at when we get to the Sullivans' home." Adam looked down at the sunglasses in his hand. *Maybe I don't have as much extra money as I thought.* He smiled when he heard Fritzy's end of the phone conversation.

"I know Mom," Fritzy paused, "but I'm here now." She glanced over at Adam. "Okay, you talk to Daddy, and I'll call you from the Sullivan house." She listened. Then to Adam, she asked, "Do you have the Sullivans' phone number handy?"

Adam pulled a piece of paper from deep inside his front pants pocket. "Let's see—Walnut 3332."

"It's Walnut 3332, Mom, in Beavertown, Ohio, just south of Dayton. Mrs. Sullivan is Mrs. Gunderman's niece. Okay—bye. I love you."

"Are they mad at me?" Adam had to ask. He was the driver, even if he didn't know Fritzy was the passenger.

"No, of course not. Mom's not too pleased with me though."

They gathered up their candy and cokes and walked out to the truck. "Do I get to ride up front with you, or should I get in the back again."

"If you'd like to ride in the back, I 'spose that would be all right." Adam climbed into the truck. "If you're going to ride up front, as short as you are, you'll probably have to crawl in."

"Here, here," she corrected him, "I'll have you know I ride in my uncle's truck a lot."

Chapter 6
Meet the Sullivans

"Let's see, Wilmington Pike, to Harvest Avenue, to Keystone," Adam said as he turned right and followed the directions.

"There it is," Fritzy said as she pointed to a light colored, yellow stucco, two story house on the left side of the road. "1524 Keystone Avenue—that's it."

"They have a dog," Adam noticed, "but I wouldn't call him a guard dog."

A black and white cocker spaniel sneezed, shook its head violently and paced back and forth across the concrete porch as Adam pulled into the driveway.

"Stop it Spotty," a girl in shorts and tee shirt said as she came out the door. "Hi, I'm Sunshine Sullivan and you must be Adam." She smiled and then looked at Fritzy.

"I must be Frederica Breman," Adam's stowaway chimed in.

"Call her Fritzy. She becomes surly if you call her Frederica," Adam joked.

"I am neither grumpy nor grouchy, Adam Schumacher," Fritzy smacked playfully on Adam's arm.

"I didn't know you were bringing a friend," Sunshine said.

"I didn't either," Adam agreed.

"Shine, is this Adam?" A woman in a cotton house dress asked through the screen door.

"Yes, Momma, and his friend, Freder—Fritzy Breman," Shine giggled. "Don't call her Frederica."

"It's not that bad, Mrs. Sullivan," Fritzy spoke as she blushed.

"Well, I am glad you're here." Grace Sullivan smiled generously as she opened the door. "Come on in. Would you two like some lemonade?"

Walking in, Adam took in the full view of the large living room. They all settled into chairs and gladly accepted frosty glasses of the cool drink. As he sipped, Adam saw a folded up studio couch and bedding stashed in the sunroom off the living room. Mr. Gunderman had been right.

"I am so glad Aunt Arletta thought of us. Did you have a good trip?" the woman asked.

"Yes, Ma'am. No problems, just a curiosity. I filled up with gas yesterday and yet the tank took a lot more than it should have a few miles back. I hope I don't have a leak in the fuel line."

"Dan won't be home for another hour or so. It's Saturday so he's working over-time today. One of our renters is an engineer and he should be coming in about that time, too. I think between the two of them they can check it out for you."

"Thanks Mrs. Sullivan. You have a nice home here," Adam said as he looked around at the living room with its sofa, three chairs, mahogany end tables and matching coffee table.

Grace seemed to watch as the two from Indiana surveyed the space. "Sunshine and her older sister usually sleep on the studio couch in the sunroom. But, Patty is staying up at their grandparent's house in Greenville this week. She won't be home for several days. Sunshine will have plenty of room in there, and Fritzy, if you want to, you can sleep there with her. Adam you can have the couch."

"If you don't mind Mrs. Sullivan, I sure would like to sleep on the glider out on the porch tonight," Adam suggested.

"Oh, I don't know. It's April, not July. Won't it be cold for you out on the porch?" Grace Sullivan said as her eyebrows lifted in surprise.

"I'm used to sleeping in a cold room, Mrs. Sullivan," Adam grinned.

"Trust me, Mrs. Sullivan, he means a very cold room," Fritzy added.

"Have you been sleeping in the barn, Adam?" Shine laughed.

"Something like that," Adam admitted. "It was the unheated belfry of our church during the Christmas holidays. But, that's another story," he said without adding more.

"I have an idea. Daddy won't be home for an hour. We usually have supper then, at four, since he goes to bed early and then gets up before the sun for work. Would you two like to play croquet until then? It's all set up." Sunshine jumped up and led the way to the screen door.

"Déjà vu," Adam sighed as he got to his feet.

"What?" Shine questioned.

"I'll translate for you. Adam is saying, 'Don't lead me around.' Déjà vu means, 'Here we go again,' because that's what I was doing...leading him around." Fritzy giggled as she grabbed hold of Adam's hand and dragged him toward the door.

"Well, excuse me," Shine bowed apologetically. "Let me ask that again. Is it possible that you might like to play a game or two of croquet before we dine? You may accompany me to the side yard if that is your desire."

"Oh Brother, there are two of them," Adam gasped and grinned. "One's just a little younger." Adam jumped up, passed the girls, bounded out the door and into the side yard with Shine and Fritzy close behind.

"Don't trip over the wickets," Shine yelled after him.

"This looks like yard-pool," Adam laughed. He picked up a mallet with blue stripes and hit a similar wooden ball around the yard from wicket to wicket beginning at the start-stake and ending at the end-stake. Once he hit the final post, he looked at his watch. "Your dad or your roomer should be home soon."

"Sometimes the renter stops and picks up his wife. She doesn't work on Saturdays so she's up in their room. Sometimes she takes the bus home." Shine looked up as the gravel between the broken concrete pieces in the driveway crackled and signaled an arrival. "Oliver Weedy doesn't talk very much, to anyone, ever."

The man drove on past the yard and pulled into the far right stall of Dan Sullivan's three car garage in his 1938 Chevy, and turned off the motor.

'Hi, Mr. Weedy," Sunshine bounced over, not too close, but close enough to get his attention. "Adam here has had a problem with his gas tank. He's missing about five gallons of gas. Can you give him any advice?"

The man slowed a little, looked in the direction of the truck and observed. "How long you been parked there?"

"An hour, maybe an hour and a half," but Adam couldn't figure what that had to do with anything? Maybe he had parked in the man's way.

"Look under the car," Weedy pointed. "You're not leaking gasoline that I can see. Are you sure you filled it up all the way?"

"Yes, sir, I am. I even rocked the truck to make sure I could get in every drop." Adam studied the driveway under the chassis—nothing.

"Someone might have siphoned it off," Weedy stated. "Five gallons will fill a five gallon, hand carried gas can, you know." With that, the man turned and carried his leather briefcase into the house.

"I always wondered about that briefcase," Sunshine said as she shook her head.

"Buddy Phillips and Freddy—"

"Alexander," Fritzy chimed in.

"Friends of yours?" Shine asked.

"No!" The two Hoosiers agreed with emphasis.

"I don't think they are even friends with each other. But, now I think I know what happened." Adam squatted down to see the full area under the Diamond T. "Mr. Weedy's right; there is no leak. On the bad side, those two hoodlums stole some hard earned gas, and on the good side, I am still getting decent gas mileage."

"Fritzy, you have a long distance telephone call," Grace called from the open kitchen window. "Better hurry."

The three young people hurried into the house and Shine pointed to the telephone. It sat on the shelf above the colonnade at the foot of the stairs that led to the rooms on the second floor. Fritzy took the receiver, sat down on a lower step, inhaled and exhaled slowly. "Hi, Momma," then she paused.

"Is there a problem?' Sunshine asked.

"Sorta," Adam answered. "Fritzy hid in the back of my truck and came along. The thing is no one knew she was leaving, including me."

"Wait a minute," Fritzy said into the receiver. "Mrs. Sullivan?" she called out.

"Yes," Grace had come into the room and sat down on an overstuffed chair, observing.

"Mom wants to talk to you, please," Fritzy held out the receiver until Grace could cross the room and take it.

"Yes?" Grace listened and then answered, "Well, I'll ask." She tuned to Sunshine. "Honey, Mrs. Breman says that Fritzy can stay here in Dayton and help Adam find his father, if you go along on the rides." Into the receiver she added, "They are welcome to sleep here, Mrs. Breman, and eat with us too—if they are here at meal time." She smiled and made sure Adam had heard her. "Do you need extra helpers, Adam?"

"That would be great, Mrs. Sullivan," Adam responded.

He smiled and sat down on the couch for a moment. The aroma of ham and beans and freshly baked corn bread floated into the room. "From the smell of dinner, I think that would be great, too."

The quest had actually begun—again. The truck would be dependable. What was even better, he would not be alone.

He had had enough of being alone in the church belfry to last a lifetime.

Chapter 7
Sunday Morning

"Adam," Sunshine poked at the blob that slept on the glider on the Sullivan's front porch. "Why did you sleep out here? Mother said you could sleep on the living room couch."

"I know. But you have the Weedys in the west two rooms upstairs and your mom's cousin, Catherine and her husband, Dave, in the east two rooms. Your parents' bedroom is in the breakfast room, you and your sister sleep on the hide-a-bed in the corner of the sunroom. If Patty hadn't been in Greenville, you would have found Fritzy curled up on the loveseat. And, I guess I'm used to sleeping in the open. You know I lived in a church belfry in the winter months." Adam smiled sheepishly, "It's a little like camping out, I guess."

"There will be a lot of us getting ready for church," Shine said. "You'd better get a move on. It's Palm Sunday you know."

Adam rubbed his eyes and stared off into the side yard. "I know. I promised Moms I'd find a church."

Sunshine patted his shoulder. "Get moving. We'll go to my church. Mother and Daddy got ready early to get out of everyone's way. Catherine and Dave got up early too and will leave soon. They'll stop for coffee at a little diner up the road. I had my bath last evening and then Fritzy took a shower. It's just you, Adam."

Adam checked his watch and jumped up. "What time do we leave?"

"Daddy will pull the car out of the garage in fifteen minutes," Shine announced as she checked her watch. "Don't worry about breakfast. Alma Garver brings homemade breakfast rolls every Sunday. She'll probably add some hot-cross buns today since it's so close to Easter."

"What are hot cross buns?" Adam asked as he rubbed his eyes.

"You've never eaten one?" Shine asked; her eyes wide. "A hot cross bun is a spiced sweet bun made with dried fruit. It's marked with a cross on the top in icing and is usually eaten during Lent."

"Can we get one before or after the service?" Adam asked with his rumbling, empty stomach in mind.

"Actually...after," she admitted. "But, if you can get a wiggle on, we can catch her before church starts. I always hurry down to the kitchen where Mrs. Garver is setting up the platters of sweet rolls. She gives me one before Mrs. Howard starts playing the prelude."

Adam lunged for the front door. "I'll be ready in ten minutes."

Sunshine laughed and followed him into the house. "It worked, Fritzy," she called into the living room.

"Food always works," Fritzy chuckled. To Adam she added, "Good morning, Mr. Schumacher."

Adam grabbed the duffle he had stashed in the corner of the living room behind a chair and darted up the steps to the one bathroom in the house. He stopped near the landing at the top and checked to make sure the bathroom door, on the other side of the hallway, was open.

•••

Beavertown E.U.B. Church sat along Wilmington Pike several miles up the road from the Sullivan home. A huge stained glass window, set into the red brick façade, faced the road. Another colorful half-circle shaped glass, channeled in lead, above the front door boasted, "Welcome." The Sullivan family, with Fritzy and Adam, all piled out of Dan Sullivan's light brown Dodge sedan in the parking lot and followed the sidewalk to the front door.

"The church looks like it's been here a long time," Fritzy marveled.

Grace stopped and admired the building. "We just celebrated our Centennial two years ago."

"Wow, the congregation started meeting in 1844?" Adam asked in amazement.

"It did," Dan Sullivan said, opened the door and stepped aside, letting his family and visitors go in first.

"This way," Sunshine directed as she hurried ahead into the vestibule and flipped around and down the circular steps that led to the Sunday School classrooms, kitchen and fellowship hall below. The basement smelled of freshly brewed coffee and something very sweet.

Adam and Fritzy were fast on Shine's heals bouncing down the grey painted steps behind her. "I can smell the rolls already," Adam swooned.

"I had breakfast," Fritzy chimed in, "but I can always eat something yummy." She playfully bumped into Adam and added, "Schumacher, you could eat a five-pound sack of sugar and not gain an ounce."

"I might try that sometime and see what happens," he said as he laughed.

"As Mother would say, 'you'd probably fly high on sweets,'" Fritzy blurted, "now that I think about it."

In the kitchen, Alma Garver was placing the last of her hot cross buns on a large glass plate. "Well, there you are Sunshine," she said and smiled. "I saved a bun for you."

"I thank you for that, Mrs. Garver. I have two friends with me. Do you by chance have two extra?" Shine asked.

"Well, now," she said as she studied the platters. "This plate looks really crowded, don't you think?"

"It does to me," Sunshine agreed. "Adam and Fritzy and I would be glad to provide more room for you. You know—a better balance for the plate."

"Thank you, my dear." Alma smiled at the three and then added, "Adam, I know boys have huge appetites. Perhaps you had better taste-test one of each kind. The cherry Danish is my favorite but, since I'm the baker, I'm partial. Perhaps you'll like the chocolate doughnuts. You can tell me if they are good enough to serve to the church family."

Adam picked up one of the flakiest pastries he had ever eaten and crumbled down his shirt. "This is great—a real home-run."

"That endorsement is good enough for me," Alma laughed as she patted Adam's cheek, puffed out from a mouthful of doughnut holes.

"Don't take too long," Shine warned them. "Church starts in a few minutes."

"Thank you, Mrs. Garver," Fritzy said as morsels of hot cross buns danced around in her mouth.

"You are welcome," Alma waved as the three started to leave the kitchen. "Sunshine," she called after her, "I saw your roomer, Oliver Weedy, the other day...in the strangest place."

The troublesome threesome stopped in mid-stride and spun around. "Where?" they asked in unison.

"That was what was so odd," she said as she rinsed crumbs from her fingers under the facet and dried them on a tea towel. "He was walking along the railroad tracks."

"The railroad tracks?" Adam asked.

"Let's go," Shine insisted and latched on to Fritzy's arm. "You grab ahold of Adam," she said as she led them out of the kitchen. In the stairway, she whispered, "I often walk on the tracks. My cousin and I used to play on the box cars, running and jumping from one car, across the gap between them, to the next one."

"Wow, that sounds dangerous," Fritzy said as she took two steps at a time, trying to keep up with Adam.

"And, we'd lay a long nail across the railroad tracks, place a second one across it, and wait for a train to pass. Then we'd collect the welded nails that now looked like little scissors."

"Gee whiz," Adam gasped. "Does your dad know you used to play on the tracks?"

"No!" she turned and put her finger up to her lips. "And, don't you tell him—Mom either."

"Right," the two Indiana teens agreed.

Sunshine stopped when she put her foot on the top step and turned to the others. "Maybe we could walk along the tracks today when it's time to go home and see if there is any obvious reason for his stroll."

"I'm tellin' your dad," a boy in bib-overalls announced from behind, then darted past them.

"You're telling him what, Allen Jeffery?" Sunshine snapped back as she grabbed the back of his shoulder straps. "I didn't tell Aunt Carolyn I caught you eating right out of the sugar bowl the last time I babysat at your house."

A.J. jerked himself away and sassed back, "Eating sugar is not the same as playing on the railroad tracks."

"It is when you stick your tongue in the sugar, A.J.," Shine insisted.

"Ignore him," Fritzy whispered as they neared the open double doors that led into the sanctuary. "The music has started."

Sunshine took the lead and wiggled in through the doors. One of the ushers was closing them just as Adam and Fritzy followed her. Shine pointed to some empty places in the third to the last row and slipped into place with the other two close on her heals.

Adam looked around the sanctuary and soaked in the colors. An arch of stained glass above the altar displayed a cross of brilliant red and blue in the center of the pane. As he turned and looked over his shoulder, he saw another window

that filled the wall, about fourteen feet high and ten feet wide in the back of the sanctuary. Four square and eight rectangular sash panes, that looked like holy documents of gold, green, red and blue supported an arch of four more panes around a half-moon semi-circle with a cross in a crown and bordered in the same jewel toned glass as the rest of the window.

"Good morning," the minister began. "God is in his holy temple. Let all the earth keep silent before him. It is wonderful to have all of you in worship this morning," he continued as he looked back at Adam, Fritzy and the Sullivan's. "I see we have some guests with us."

"Yes, Dr. Kennedy," Fritzy offered. "I'd like you to meet our house guests, Adam Schumacher and Frederica, Fritzy, Breman. They're from Indiana."

Adam waved at A.J. when the boy turned around and stared at the Hoosier twosome. He pointed a finger of warning authority at him. A.J. slumped in the pew.

The Palm Sunday service was similar to the one at the church he and Fritzy attended back in Middletown. Children brought in palm branches and placed them at the foot of the altar as a middle-aged man sang the solo, The Palms. It was a service of joy and triumphant entry into Jerusalem, the arrival of the King of Love and peace.

After the service, the congregation gathered in an adjacent Sunday school classroom where a table loaded with hot cross buns and other pastries, coffee and punch waited. Adam managed to eat two more of the iced treats. He could have eaten more but didn't want to appear to be a glutton. Full, but not stuffed, they walked out the tall front doors of the church.

"Hey, A.J., wait up a minute, friend," Adam called to the boy.

"Pastor introduced you in church today, but that doesn't mean you're my friend." A.J. closed his eyes, stuck out his tongue, put his thumbs in his ears and wiggled his hands back and forth.

"You are a safe and wise kid, A.J.," Adam said as he smiled back and ignored the childish face. "I have a business proposition for you."

"Huh, business?" the boy asked. "I'm already in business. I get ten cents for picking up sticks in the yard before Dad mows."

"That sounds good," Adam encouraged. "Of course you have the privilege of playing in the yard so...seems to me like that's payment enough."

"Hey, I've got a good thing going here," A.J. protested.

"Now that's where we can help each other," Adam said and patted the boy on the shoulder. "You won't tell Sunshine's father about her walking along the railroad tracks, and I won't tell your dad about the new law, XYZ-Subsection Tango." He smiled as he thought about his long days working on the farm, planting corn, bailing hay and taking care of the animals. He didn't consider it work. He loved his time working with Pops.

"What? What's that XYZ thing?" A.J. asked while Fritzy and Shine looked away, trying to stifle grins that threatened to spread.

"Law XYZ is about workers who are employed in people's homes. Subsection Tango concerns payments to children."

A.J.'s eyes grew large and his mouth, shaped in a perpetual gasp, hung open.

Adam continued, "The government doesn't believe that parents should pay their children for work around their home since the kids benefit from a clean home and a yard cleared of dangerous obstacles." He didn't pause but kept his fabricated story going in full motion. "Now, A.J., we certainly don't want to interfere with your job as lawn keeper. So—we'll help you if you help us."

"How?" A.J. asked with a look of curiosity mixed with fear of early retirement.

"I'm talking about an agreement of silence," he stated very professionally while A.J. stared at him.

"Silence?"

Adam moved closer as others came out of the church. "Law XYZ is new. Not everyone knows about it yet. So, we won't tell anyone about it and, as I said, you won't tell Sunshine's father about the railroad tracks. Maybe they won't publish information about the XYZ Law until you're in college and away from the twigs in your yard. You can continue to earn your ten cents, and Shine can continue to take the short cut home. Agreed?"

"Yeah, I agree," A.J. said and grinned as he eagerly shook Adam's hand.

"Thanks man." Adam started to leave, but turned back. "Don't forget to give ten percent to the church."

"Ten percent? I'm just in the third grade."

"That would be a penny off every dime you earn."

The grin on A.J.'s face spread from cheek to cheek until it completely covered his face. "A penny? Great. Thanks Adam."

"Sure enough, big guy," Adam said as they started down the steps to the sidewalk. "Working men have to stick together—like our own union of family out-door workers."

Chapter 8
Walking Home

"Mom," Sunshine called over her shoulder when she saw her parents come out the church door, "we're going to walk home."

"All right," Grace answered. "Make sure you're home by lunch time. We're having pot roast."

"Just like in Middletown," Fritzy said and smiled.

"I'm hungry already," Adam chimed in. "I think every mid-western mom in the United States puts rich browned roast beef in the oven, with potatoes and carrots, before they leave for church on Sunday morning." He closed his eyes for a second and thought about Sunday dinner on the farm. "I really am hungry just thinking about lunch."

Shine stopped and shook her head. "Adam, you had a Danish roll, doughnut holes and a hot cross bun before church and two more after services. How can you be hungry?"

Fritzy laughed. "He's a boy."

"Okay, 'boy'—see if you can keep up," Shine challenged him as she increased her pace and the length of her stride. She was down the front sidewalk and had turned right before Adam had finished wiping his fingers on his handkerchief.

Next door to the church, the smell of grain and alfalfa oozed out between the cracks around the windows and under the door of the closed feed store. It reminded Adam of the barn on the farm. The red bank-barn in the yard next to his family's house was a county beauty, with a grassy slope that led to the tall double barn doors. One of his jobs was to fill the feed troughs and throw fresh hay and straw down from the haymow to the animals below. He wondered how anything could smell like fresh air as he inhaled deeply there in the city. He hurried past the little store with multi-pane windows and tried not to think of home or Moms and Pops. The sweet earthy smell of animal feed made him so homesick, he felt tears trying to burst through the protective dam he had fortified. He didn't think he could hold them back.

"Devon Avenue?" Fritzy questioned as they turned right at the next corner. She skipped a little around the corner, speeding up to catch up. "I thought your house was straight ahead on Wilmington Pike and then turn right."

"It is," Shine answered and continued along the sidewalk. "We can take a short cut on the railroad tracks and see if there is anything out of the ordinary at the same time."

"Where's the railroad tracks from here?" Adam asked as he followed her. There was no train ahead and she did say, "short cut."

Shine smiled and said, "You're used to being in the lead aren't you, Schumacher—in control?"

Adam stammered and raked his fingers through his hair. "I don't know about that."

"Adam is an only child," Fritzy said as she came to his rescue. "That should explain it all."

"Okay," Adam said as he attempted to redirect the conversation and resign the role of piñata at a birthday party. "It looks like a school up ahead. Where to now?"

Shine hurried up to a little creek, stopped at the bridge rail, picked up a pebble off the sidewalk and tossed it in. "I always drop a little stone in the water just to see how deep it is." She studied the water below for a second. "It's deep enough."

"For what?" Adam asked as he looked over the side at the little stream of ambling water.

"My cousin and I used to sail small sailboats on the creek when I was little," Shine said. "I don't anymore, but I always want to know if the water is deep enough if I would ever want to sail a boat."

"The railroad tracks, Shine?" Adam asked impatiently. "Where are the tracks?" He pulled away from the bridge railing and walked on toward the school.

"The train tracks are on the other side of Pasadena Grade School over there," Shine pointed to a long row of higher grass on the other side of the school. "We'll go around this end of the school and cut through the playground and baseball diamond," she said. "My Uncle Bill went to school there, too." She led the others as they darted across the little side street in front of the school, around the end of the building, sprinted past the swings and slides and cut through the ball field. "Here we are," she said as she walked the few steps through the taller grasses that ran parallel to the tracks.

"Great," Adam exhaled with relief as he walked onto the tracks and started walking south. "Let's see if we can find anything that would tell us what Weedy was up to when Mrs. Garver saw him on the tracks. His brown leather wing-tips don't look like the kind of shoes for hiking. There has to be something else."

"Look who's in the lead now," Fritzy giggled as she tugged on the back of Adam's shirt.

"Never mind, Breman," Adam warned, partly irritated and mostly teasing.

"Yes, sir," she taunted playfully.

They trudged along the railroad tracks, sometimes walking on the iron rails using them as a balance beam, other times skipping from cross tie to cross tie. The spring air and the music of the birds made the mile walk worth every step.

"Here," Sunshine announced as she stepped off the tracks not far from her home.

"Here? Where?" Fritzy asked. "That's just an overgrown thicket it seems to me."

Adam looked around at the topsy-turvy vines, thorn bushes, and twisted tree roots. "It looks more like an entrance to a hobbit-hole than a hiding place for any clue Weedy might have left."

"Well," Shine said, "it kinda is an overgrown thicket." She kept walking down off the tracks and crossed a dry burr-weed overgrown ditch. "Mrs. Garver said she saw him when she drove down Roslyn Avenue. That street is right over there." She pointed to the street that ran parallel to the tracks in a stretch not far from the Sullivan house.

Fritzy pulled up her skirt and waded through the grass. "Good grief, what a mess. I don't want burrs all over my clothes. If I had my boots, this would be fun."

"So you're an explorer, too?" Shine asked.

Adam fanned out to the right, trying to cover as much ground as possible. "She can keep up with me and that's saying a lot." He looked over at Fritzy and smiled, then quickly looked away when he felt his face grow hot. Strange, he had never blushed before when he looked at Fritzy. Why now? He fixed his eyes straight ahead and kept on moving.

When Sunshine got to the top of a dirt mound, she reached down and dusted some lumpy dirt from the top then brushed her hands together. "This is what I wanted to show you guys." Looping her finger through a pull-ring, she tugged on a warn brass finger loop and slowly lifted the heavy trap door. Dust and dirt scattered in the air causing a foggy effected that blurred their view. All three of them sputtered as they leaned over the opening in the mound and peered into the dug-out.

"What is this place?" Adam gasped as he choked on the stale air from below. They all coughed and held their breath, blocking the rotten odor that wafted up.

"I'm just guessing," Shine said as she looked down into the dark cavern, "but I think the guy who lives down the street, Rob Roberts, and his friends built this vertical cave several years ago. He's five years older than I am and graduated already. He lives near here, so I think he and his cronies dug it out."

"Let's climb in," Adam announced, sat down on the edge and dropped through the opening into a cave-like structure dug out of a huge dirt hill covered with weeds.

"Move over," Fritzy said, "I'm coming down." She dropped into the underground boy-cave and wrinkled up her nose. "It stinks in here, and it's littered with trash. It smells like they forgot to build in a bathroom."

"Why would Weedy come into a dump like this?" Shine asked as she lowered herself down through the opening.

"He wouldn't," Adam whispered in deep thought. "All the more reason he might have been here."

"What?" Shine asked. "That doesn't make any sense."

"Sure it does," Fritzy agreed. "He could hide something down here in all this junk and no one would think to follow him in here. It's a perfect hiding place for him: no frills, no polish, and no tweed."

"Exactly," Adam stated. "Let's look around and then get out of here."

Shine raised both hands in surrender. "Good honk, what are we looking for?"

Adam picked up a stick from the pounded dirt floor and slowly started separating the random pieces of garbage. "Look for anything that doesn't look like trash."

"When you find another stick, let me know." Fritzy gagged as she pulled back some rat gnawed, moldy food. "It may have been bread in a previous life," she shuddered.

"Make that two sticks," Shine added. "I don't want to touch anything. That makes it hard to look below the first layer of rubbish."

"This is taking my appetite away really fast," Fritzy moaned. "And, that pot roast sounded so good." She patted her stomach. "How can you feel hungry and not want to put anything in your mouth?"

"It's called being in high school," Adam drew out slowly as he fixed his eyes on the floor and stirred.

Sunshine put her hands in her skirt pockets, trying to avoid coming into contact with anything. Searching with her eyes only, she bent over and looked under a rickety old table painted in a flaky green paint. "What's that under there?" she asked as she studied something from several angles. "It doesn't look old. It looks like it doesn't belong here."

Adam reached far under the table with the help of his stick and pulled out a sheet of heavy blue paper with staples across the top and small bits of papers protruding from the wire fasteners. "It looks like something was torn off."

"It doesn't make any sense now," Fritzy said as she pulled an old box over beneath the opening. "It might later and…since that is the only out-of-place piece of evidence down here, let's take it with us." She studied the box placement below the opening. "So, I'm done. I'm going back to the Sullivan house."

"Me, too," Shine said. "We can always come back if we need to, but I think my lungs will burst if I stay down here any longer. I'll show you the way."

"I'll touch it and carry it out of here," Adam waved the paper between his fingers. "It's not as disgusting as everything else down here."

They each used the crate Fritzy found to make it easier to climb out of the dug-out. Once out and on top of the mound in the beautiful rays of the sun, each one stopped and filled their lungs with fresh air. Shine faced eastwardly and pointed. "See, Keystone Avenue dead-ends right over there. Our house is just up the street."

"Great," Adam exhaled slowly. "The first thing I want to do when we get to your house is wash my hands, maybe three or four times."

Shine put out her hand to stop Adam and Fritzy. "Wait a minute. It's best if Mother and Daddy don't know anything about this," she said. She pointed out a path and started walking in the direction of the house.

"They already know we walked home," Adam reminded her.

Shine smiled sheepishly. "I know. But—they don't know about my shortcut on the railroad tracks or Rob's dug-out."

"Exploring isn't for the timid…or for parents," Adam agreed. As they neared the front porch of the Sullivan home, he thought he could smell the rich flavor of the roast beef.

Compared to the dug-out, it smelled like his mother's perfume that waited for her in a fancy little bottle on her dresser at the farm house. Home, and all the aromas that went with it, filled his senses until there was nothing left of the ugliness. His taste buds were primed and ready for what lay ahead.

Chapter 9
Wrens and a Hummingbird

Sunday dinner sat on the dining room table when Adam and the girls walked in. Grace had spread a colorful red flowered table cloth under the serving dishes and place settings.

"Oh good, you're here," she said to the three as they came in. "We'll need milk or water poured in the glasses and the bread plate is still in the kitchen." When she looked at their hands her mouth flew open in surprise. "Oh my! Wash your hands at the kitchen sink before you touch any food or sit at the table."

"Sure Mama," Sunshine agreed.

Grace turned and put her hand on her hip. "Where were you three that you got so dirty?"

Adam looked at Shine and offered, "We took a short cut through the field." This of course was partially true. After all, they had walked through the weeds at the end of Keystone Avenue before coming out on the paved road.

"Gracious," Grace said again. "Well, hurry and wash up."

Shine led the way through the swinging door into the kitchen. She pushed the door against the wall and pointed to the sink. "There's soap there on the tray. I'll get a hand towel out of the cabinet."

The kitchen was very modest with a wall mounted porcelain sink and a Frigidaire stove. A small span of blue linoleum-covered counter top was under the window with two small upper cabinets and a Frigidaire refrigerator at the end of the counter. "Daddy works at the Frigidaire," Shine explained.

"Wow, you sure are lucky," Adam said as he thought about the sparse kitchen on the farm with the wood burning stove that Moms would use with artistic skill to create their Sunday family dinners. He waited for the girls to finish washing up then ran the warm water over his hands and lathered up with the bar of Lux soap.

Shine walked over to the refrigerator. "I'll get out Mama's grape jelly and butter. Fritzy, you get the bread from over there on the counter. Adam, when you finish washing up, come on in."

Adam washed his hands and then followed the girls into the dining room. Dan Sullivan sat at the head of the table; Grace was at the foot, in the end chair near the kitchen door.

"Adam, you and Fritzy sit on this side of the table." Grace pointed to the side opposite the kitchen. "Sunshine sits on this side."

"Let's pray," Dan said as he bowed his head. He thanked God for the food and the blessings they had already received. He also thanked God for Adam and Fritzy's visit. "Amen."

"Pass whatever is in front of you," Grace instructed, unfolded her napkin and placed it in her lap.

"It all looks great, Gracie," Dan said in a mildly southern accent.

"Oliver spoke to me before he and Evelyn went out for lunch," Grace said as she spooned potato chunks, absorbed in rich broth, onto her plate. "He said they finally found a house in Miamisburg."

"Miamisburg? Why down there?" Shine asked as she pulled her piece of chuck roast apart with her fork.

"They can afford to eat out on Sunday morning?" Fritzy asked.

"He has a really good job. It was a lack of available housing after the war that caused a problem for them," Grace answered. "That's why they were looking for a house in Miamisburg. Oliver works for the government, and they will be building something called Mound Laboratories there in the next year or two. Buying a home in Miamisburg will give the Weedys a head start on the home market."

"Weedy works for the government?" Adam asked as he put his fork down and laced his fingers together with his elbows resting on the table. "Oh," he stopped and pulled his elbows back, "sorry."

"You're okay. Be comfortable, son," Dan smiled as he placed both forearms on the edge of the table and leaned in.

Adam relaxed his posture but didn't stop thinking of Oliver Weedy and his government job. Maybe he could find out more about it if he asked the right questions.

"After dinner," Dan began, "I'm wonderin' if you'd help me, Adam. With Weedy still out for the day, I can easily get to his side of the garage."

"Sure, what ya need?"

"The wren houses way up high near the top of the two story garage. They're bein' invaded."

"Wren houses?" Adam asked.

"You know, little birds," Fritzy filled in.

Adam stared back with a cocked head. "I know what a wren is...Frederica," he enunciated distinctly.

Fritzy stuck out her tongue and smiled. "What's the problem with the wren houses? I'll help."

"Okay then, we'll go check it out." Dan folded his napkin and placed it beside his plate.

"I'll help Mom with the dishes," Shine offered and then laughed. "Let me know if the tiny birds attack. I'll come to the rescue."

"Sounds jake," Adam said as he jumped up and followed.

The spring afternoon was warm and breezy, just the kind of day that made Adam feel at home and homesick at the same time. They crunched across some broken concrete pieces in the driveway until they got to the three garage doors. Dan grabbed the chrome handle on the far right stall, pulled it down and lifted the door.

Inside the old carriage building, the smell gave away the presence of dead mice that probably lived in the corners. The sun shone through the multi-paned windows in the two end peaks of the rafters and cast beams across the concrete floor.

"There they are," Fritzy said as she pointed to the little bird houses high off the ground.

"I've got a ladder over here," Dan talked as he walked to the corner of the open studded structure and retrieved a very tall wooden set of rung steps.

"I'll grab the end," Adam offered as he helped pull the very large ladder from where it leaned.

"What can I do?" Fritzy asked.

"We're gonna lean the ladder against the wall right there under the bird house," Dan said as he picked up his side and groaned.

"Are you all right, sir?" Adam asked as he watched Shine's dad struggle.

"Sure, I'm okay," he said. His mouth tightened into a strained pout. "Fritzy, if you'll clear away that newspaper Weedy dropped; the ladder won't slip on it."

"Yep, will do," Fritzy agreed. Hopping into position, she whisked it off the floor.

Dan put his foot on the bottom rung and grabbed each side of the ladder. "Now, Adam, you grab hold of it and steady the thing while I go up and see what's goin' on. See there on the floor? There's another baby bird that's fallen outa the nest."

"The bird sure is little," Adam observed.

"It's a Carolina wren, Dave Reynolds, Catherine's husband, said," Dan explained. "They're really small."

"But...fallen?" Fritzy asked. "Do they fall very often?"

"Never." Dan went up a few more steps. "They're birds. They shouldn't fall from the nest. That's the third one I've seen on the floor. That's why I wanna see what's goin' on." As he looked up, white bird poop dropped from the nest and landed on his forehead and dripped down his cheek. "Yuck!" he yelled in surprise and disgust. Startled and closing his eyes to avoid contamination, his feet slipped and he stumbled off the ladder.

"Mr. Sullivan!" Adam gasped as he grasped at him to steady his balance. "Are you okay?"

"Yeah," Dan grumbled as he reached over and jerked a shop-rag that hung on the wall from a nail. "I have been greatly insulted by a tiny bird," he spit out, wiping his face again and again. Then, he started to laugh and threw his head back. "I don't think Gracie will let me in the house like this. I'll havta run the water hose over my head."

"Let me go up, sir," Adam offered as he got into position at the bottom of the ladder.

"You wanna be baptized in bird droppin's, too?" Dan asked and laughed again.

"Here, Adam," Fritzy offered. "I found this gardening hat on the work bench over there against the wall."

"That's Gracie's," Dan said. "But, she don't like to garden, so that should be just fine. Put it on, Adam."

Fritzy plopped the wide brimmed straw hat on Adam's head and started to tie the pink ribbons under his chin.

"Not the bow!" Adam complained loudly.

"It will fall off when you look up if I don't tie it," Fritzy insisted.

"Okay, okay," Adam moaned. Jerking the ribbons out of Fritzy's hands, he tied the bow himself.

Fritzy smiled with a twinkle in her eye. "Very fetching," she said as she stifled a giggle.

Adam batted his eyes, pretending to be shy, "Thank you so much," he whispered. He started up the ladder, looking down at each foot placement and up at the bird house. Just then, another baby wren fell out of the little round opening in the side of the wren house. The opening was small enough a sparrow or large bird could not get in. High above the garage floor, Adam reached out his hand and caught the wren in mid-air with his right hand and held on tightly to the ladder with his left.

Fritzy quickly took a handkerchief from her pocket. "I'll take it," she offered as she started up the ladder. "If I keep it in my hankie, the momma bird might take it back."

With his hair still dripping with bird dirt, Dan untucked his shirt and wiped his face again on his undershirt. "The handkerchief's a good idea," he said. "I've always heard, momma birds don't come back to a disturbed nest." He inspected his shirt and added, "Mommas don't want dirty birds back in the nest either." Dan wiped his eyes with the back of his hand and headed out to the garden hose.

Adam continued up the ladder until he reached the wren house. Studying the small structure without touching it, he looked it over, above, under and peered inside. A beady bird eye stared at him and then twisted its head back and forth to get a look with the other eye. "The mother is in here," Adam called down to those below.

"The mother bird pushed the babies out?" Fritzy's voice rose to a squeak in surprise. "Why would she do that?"

"I'm not sure she thought much about it," Adam said with a laugh. He quickly stopped as a long beak protruded from the wren house opening. "Well, hello there," he greeted.

"Who? What?" Fritzy asked.

Dan stopped hosing off his head at the yard faucet beside the garage door and darted back in the car stall. "What'd you find?"

Adam stuck his finger carefully and slowly in through the round opening in the wren house. When he pulled his hand steadily back out, a small ruby throated hummingbird was perched on his finger.

"Rudy?" Fritzy squealed.

Adam rhythmically turned the red and green feathered hummer around a little to get a good look. "No...I wish he was," he sighed. "I set Rudy free last winter."

"Rudy?" Dan asked.

Adam spoke softly and gently. "When I was living in the belfry of our church last Christmas, a little hummer postponed his winter migration just to keep me company. I don't think I would have made it without him. I called him Rudy."

Fritzy smiled as she remembered the conversation she already had with Adam about Rudy. "Daddy said hummingbirds fly all the way to Mexico for the winter. Even though they need flower nectar frequently throughout the day, they soar above the waters of the Gulf of Mexico for long distances."

"Remember, Adam," Fritzy reminded him, "the Native Americans say that a hummingbird symbolizes timeless joy and the Nectar of Life."

"You told me that, and I almost forgot. So that's what the Indians say, is it?" Adam said as he smiled.

"It is," she agreed. "The hummingbird is a symbol for accomplishing things which seem impossible."

Adam watched the hummer in his hand and added, "I have plenty of *impossible* ahead of me," he sighed and then brightened. "People believe hummers fly south on the backs of northern geese. Some stories say they fly piggyback under the geese's wings."

Dan paused and asked, "Ain't it amazin' how God provides for our needs when we need them? You needed a lot, and God chose to give you company to fight your loneliness first. He knew your deepest need."

"Yes, he did," Adam admitted. "And, he knows this hummer's needs. He wasn't tossing the baby birds out. He got into the wren house and then couldn't get out. He caught his wing on the side of the opening. As he flopped around in there, the baby wrens got evicted."

"The hummer must be mighty hungry," Dan guessed. "Now, God is usin' you to meet the needs of Rudy the Second, right here and now. Ain't life wonderful?" He paused and watched Adam release the hummingbird into the trees of the yard. "What's your greatest need today, Adam?"

Adam, Fritzy and Sunshine's trips around Dayton

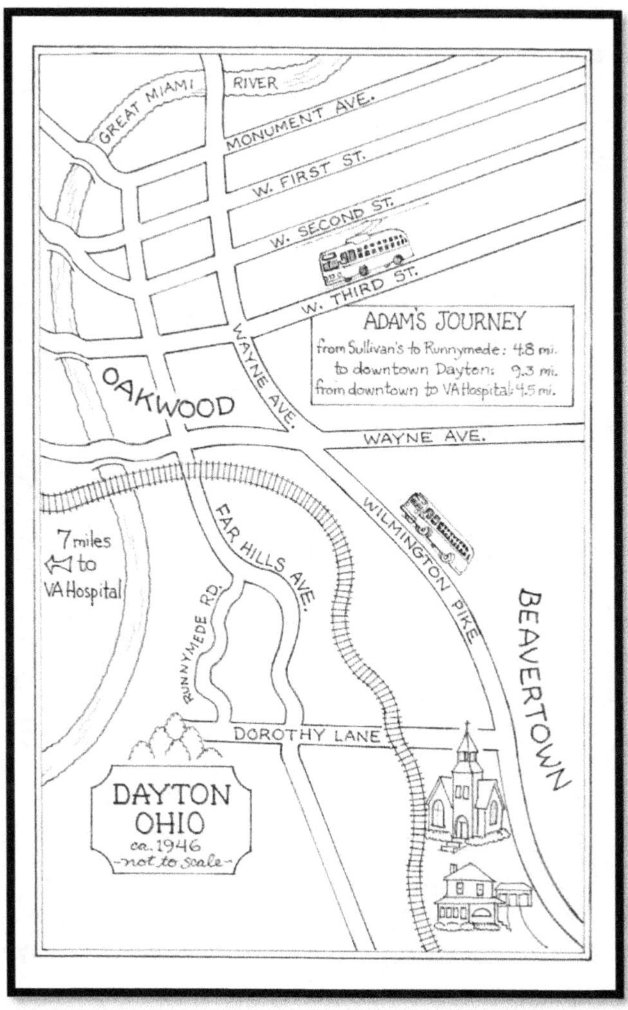

84

Chapter 10
Monday Morning

The sun had already brightened the side yard enough to cast multi-hues of green across the grass. In Adam's half-awake fog, shadows of light were a welcome relief from apparitions of ghostly gremlins and goblins.

Shine came out of the house, sat down on one of the porch chairs and started talking before Adam was awake enough to know what she was talking about. "Mother doesn't drive," she said, "so she can't take us into the VA, and Daddy has gone to work. We'll take the bus into town and then transfer to a cross town line."

"Sounds good to me." Adam rubbed his eyes while his stomach growled and rumbled.

"Oh, right—breakfast," Shine announced with a chuckle. "Mom has scrambled eggs ready and toast is being buttered. Fold up the blanket and come on in."

Adam looked out on the lawn as the morning sun quickly commanded the day. Tulips had opened in little clusters beside full blooming peony bushes. The scent of the large pink blossoms drifted up to the porch and hovered over the glider. Adam thought of Moms, stood up and folded the blanket.

Bang, the screen door slammed shut as Oliver Weedy dashed out. "Oh, hi, sorry young man," Weedy said and kept going.

"Good morning, sir," Adam greeted the man he had met Saturday afternoon. As they passed, Adam shrugged. "A busy day, I guess," Adam offered politely.

"Always busy, always on the move," Weedy chuckled.

"What do you do?" Adam asked the man who never stopped long enough to meet him eye to eye. He hoped to get a clearer answer than simply, "a government worker."

Weedy stopped but didn't turn around. "I work with some... secret papers, son. Can't talk about it."

"Oh, sure. Sorry I asked." Adam watched the man hurry on in the direction of the garage.

"Have a good day," Weedy waved his briefcase in the air without stopping.

Adam started to open the front door, when Evelyn Weedy grabbed the handle. "Sorry again," he laughed. "I seem to be in the wrong place this morning," he apologized.

"What?" she questioned without stopping.

"I nearly ran into your husband already this morning. Now you, too," Adam called after her as she hurried down the steps. Her husband had just backed out of his stall of the garage and waited in the drive at the bottom of the steps. Evelyn walked around the car, jerked the door open, and got in without another word.

Adam watched them pull out of the driveway onto the street, and went in the house. The aroma of crisp bacon and toast floated in from the kitchen. "Hi, you two."

Fritzy and Sunshine sat at the dining room table sipping tall glasses of orange juice. Adam pulled out a chair, picked up his glass and swirled the juice around until the thick, plump pulp stuck to the rim.

"Looks like you slept pretty good," Fritzy said. "Your hair sticks up only on one side. Didn't you move all night?"

"Actually, I did," he smiled and raked his fingers over the top of his head.

"So, what is the plan for today?" Mrs. Sullivan asked as she brought in plates with a large spoonful of scrambled eggs in the middle of each.

Adam smiled. The mound stood up on his plate and reminded him of his mother's best fluffy-eggs. Scenes of family breakfasts, before Pops went off to the war, flashed through his mind. He shook his head, trying to chase the thoughts away. It reminded him of cleaning out the barn with a large pitch fork.

"We're going to go over to the VA and try to get a lead on my father," Adam answered as he stuck his fork in the pile of pale yellow eggs.

"About what time will you be home?" Grace asked.

"We'll be back by dinner time." Shine tore a piece of toast in half and bit a huge chunk out of the soft middle.

Mrs. Sullivan sat down and began to eat. "Give me a call if you're late."

With that request, the plans only waited execution. Sunshine had permission to travel all over Dayton and the surrounding area as long as the bus and/or trolley line could take her there and bring her safely back—on time.

An hour later, on a beautiful Ohio day in the spring of 1946, Adam, Fritzy and Sunshine walked the block and a half to the bus stop on the corner up on Wilmington Pike. It was far too early in the year for the little vegetable stand across the street from the stop to be open, but the large horizontal shutter was up. Inside, a small woman was dusting shiny metal scales and wiping off the counter. She waved at Shine and said something that Adam could not understand.

"She's deaf," Sunshine whispered as she covered her mouth slightly. "But, she hears a little, so she reads lips, uses sign language, and speaks some. I know she's hard to understand. Her husband is completely deaf. They have two sons who hear just fine. Mr. and Mrs. Gladding are great people. If they're going into town when I'm waiting at the bus stop, they take me in. I love to watch them from the backseat of the car as they talk to each other with their hands."

"Good morning, Mrs. Gladding," Shine hollered, careful to over-enunciate her words. "It's a beautiful day."

"Yes, it is," the woman called back using words that had fuzzy consonants.

"Have you seen anything strange this morning?" the girl asked clearly.

"Not this morning. Everything is as usual." Mrs. Gladding removed the scales from the narrow counter, and placed them someplace under the shelf.

"Bye," Sunshine waved as the bus approached, passing Dicken's Market about a half block farther up the road. To Adam she added, "Both of the Gladdings may not be able to hear, but they see everything."

Adam shook his head in amazement. He had never been around people who couldn't hear. They seemed to ignore their deafness and live their days in their own way.

When the bus stopped, Adam and the girls climbed up the three steps, dropped their coins in the cash box next to the driver and listened as the money clattered along the shoots that fed to the bottom of the glass box. Finding seats near the back of the bus, they sat down, with Adam and Fritzy on a center-facing bench seat and Sunshine on the end of the long front-facing bench next to them in the back.

Shine explained the travel plan. "We'll ride this bus all the way into Dayton and then transfer to a west-bound bus. The VA Hospital is about six or seven miles out on West Third Street from downtown." She looked at the advertising posters along the top of the bus, in the curved area near the ceiling.

"I bet you have each of those advertisements and pictures memorized," Adam said out loud.

Shine smiled. "I ride buses all over Dayton—to the roller skating rink, the movies, shopping in the stores downtown."

"This ride is great," Fritzy beamed as she admired the passing houses with their beautiful lawns beyond the windows, and the clean and friendly atmosphere on board the bus. "I wish we had a public bus system in our town. It sure would be easy to get around."

"Do you think Coach would let his daughter run around like Sunshine's parents do?" Adam laughed.

Shine adjusted her jacket and squared her back. "My parents tell me they want me to learn to be independent."

"My dad wants me to be independent, too," Fritzy agreed, "as long as he knows where I am all the time."

"That's because you're such a mischief-makers," Adam teased.

"What about you, Adam?" their new friend asked. "What do your parents expect from you?"

"My dad never came home from the war, remember? That's who we're trying to find." His tone was edgy and clipped. "I haven't spoken to him in years. I wouldn't have any idea what my Pops would want for me."

"Wow," Fritzy explained, "that's more words than I've heard out of you in a long time."

"Sorry," Shine sighed. "That was my fault. I wasn't thinking. My father wasn't in the war. He had been hurt in an industrial accident and still limps a little."

Adam relaxed his muscles and flexed his neck. "That's okay. I know you just forgot." Then he added quietly, "Moms was in a tuberculosis sanitarium for the last...nearly a year. We were just able to move her to a friend's apartment after Christmas." He thought for a moment. "I'm sorry to hear about your father."

"That's okay," Shine said as she picked at her fingernails. She added, "The apartment sounds nice."

"The Gundermans are great people," Fritzy joined in.

Sunshine looked out the windows and offered her expertise as a travel guide. "That building over there is the Oakwood Library," she said as they passed a red brick building on the right. Green ivy vines crawled up the walls like tiny climbing ropes ready for a full military breech of the castle. Further north, they passed beautifully settled homes built in the 1920's and 30's, that sprawled out across manicured lawns. Old movies were full of heroines carrying wide brimmed hats on yards such as these. "Orville Wright lives down there," Shine pointed.

"The inventor of the airplane?" Adam gasped.

"Yes, of course," Shine stated. She was used to traveling about town and coming near the great and famous. "Go west to Harman Avenue and continue through where Park Avenue crosses. There's a large Southern style colonial house on your left the Wrights called Hawthorne Hill because they lived on Hawthorne Street when they lived in Dayton. Orville and his sister, Katherine, and their father live there."

"Gosh," Adam gasped, both at the nearness to greatness and Sunshine's freedom to investigate her hometown.

As the bus started down Far Hills Avenue, the view of the city stretched out before them. "What is all of that?" Adam asked about the many blond brick buildings that sprouted up at the foot of the hill before getting to the city proper.

"All of those buildings are the National Cash Register Company," Shine smiled with pride. "They've made cash registers here since 1884. Some of my uncles work here."

"That's a really big place," Adam said as they passed the buildings that stood on both sides of the street.

"I go there on the bus with friends on Saturdays for their free movie for any kid in town who can get there," Shine said with the lilt of pride in her voice. "At Christmas, they run two shows and give a box of candy and a silver dollar to everyone. There are thousands that go at Christmas."

"Wow," the two out-of-towners admired in unison.

South Main Street started where Far Hills left off, under the railroad over-pass, and proceeded into the commercial and retail district of Dayton.

"That's Elders and Johnson's Department Store on the left," Shine pointed. "Rikes, another great store, is a few blocks up on the corner of Second and Main Streets. Mama took me to Rikes when I was still in the baby buggy. We couldn't ride the escalator with the buggy wheels and all; but, the moving stairs have always been my favorite way of moving up, over the elevator. My preference probably began when we couldn't ride it. I don't like to be told, 'No'," she said as she smiled with determination.

"I never would have guessed," Adam snickered.

As they cleared the next intersection, the Court House stood alone in the next block, with banks, small business and the Home Store on the right.

"Dunbar High School," Shine pointed to a massive, dark old gothic looking school building on the right. "It was named after the black poet, Paul Laurence Dunbar, a classmate and friend of Orville Wright." She was silent for a few minutes and then popped up, "This is our stop."

Adam and Fritzy scrambled to their feet, fell in step behind Sunshine and stepped off the bus in the middle of town. The city was alive with the hum of cars, trucks and other buses, all angling for the same piece of space on Main Street. The three young people watched the bus move on north.

"Behind those stores," Shine pointed to the businesses that faced Main Street, across the street and down a block, "is the amazing Arcade." She started walking to the corner with Adam and Fritzy close behind. "We have a little time before the cross-town trolley gets here. Let me show it to you."

"Arcade?" Adam asked as he stopped and frowned. "As in...the midway at the county fair...where the games are?"

"No," Shine laughed. "As in...a covered walkway with stores on both sides." As she briskly led the way down the wide city sidewalk to the corner, a man in a fedora hat jumped out of the passenger side of a sedan and locked step in behind them. Adam and his friends took no notice.

Shine, Adam and Fritzy waited for the light to change and then ran across the street. "In here," Shine called out as she pulled on one of the double glass doors that opened at the Third Street entrance. Inside, a long hallway covered in hexagon shaped white tiles with black trim, provided a dry walkway for the stores that flanked the arcade corridor.

To the right was an elegant jewelry and gift shop with dark mahogany display cases and light blue carpeting. A large gold gilded clock sat on one of the tables, with etched crystal figurines encircling it. The colors stimulated Adam but it was too high-class for his comfort. Still, Grams had always said, "Hold your head up high, look people in the eye, and you will belong anywhere."

A brightly lit camera store was on the left of the glass hallway, stocked with some photography equipment Adam had never seen before. He scanned every long lens and fitted camera case in the store as they hurried on. Walking past, Adam caught a glimpse of a man in a hat pausing at their every stop. "Who?" he asked as he spun around. But, all he could see was the back of a man as he darted into one of the shops.

"Who...what?" Fritzy asked as she looked around.

Adam searched up and down the hall and shrugged. "No one I guess."

At the end of the hall, they crossed into a room of magic. The huge space was circular in shape with an open market on the first floor, topped by a glass-domed rotunda, seventy feet high and ninety feet in diameter. Below the dome and above the ground level there were two balconied upper floors that circled the central farmers' market.

Shine smiled when she saw the amazement on Adam's face. "The balconies open into private apartments, offices, and small businesses."

"I cannot imagine living in the city," Adam groaned. "I don't mean the suburbs like where you live, Shine. I mean the *city*."

"Wow," Fritzy stared in amazement. "I think living here would be the boss."

"I'll admit," Adam stated reluctantly, "it might be super to live above businesses, like McCrory's Five and Ten." He looked around at all the doors that opened into colorful stores. "Moms would love to live above a beauty parlor or dress shop. And look, the floor of the rotunda has about fifty food market vendors. She could buy fish, flowers, and meat right here below her back door." He smiled broadly. "Moms would have life a whole lot easier than it is now. The Liberal Super Market is right over there," he gestured in the direction of double green doors.

Shine grinned as she twirled around, taking in every bit of the place, as if she'd never seen it before. "I love this place. The balconies above open into private apartments. And, over there," she pointed, "is a horseshoe shaped lunch counter that serves the best fountain cokes in Dayton." She checked her watch and jumped. "Golly, gee whiz, we'd better hurry. The trolley will be here in a few minutes."

Adam and the girls hurried out of the Arcade into the bright sunlight. As they dashed along the sidewalk, Adam caught the shadow of a man who followed them out. He then jumped into a sedan waiting at the curb. It was the same man Adam had seen earlier, he was sure. He brushed the image of the man aside and thought no more of it.

Shine hustled them back to Main Street. There, they crossed to the other side, opposite the Court House, where South Main became North Main. Pausing at the trolley stop, they regrouped to continue their trip across town.

While they stood there waiting, Shine pointed to the parallel electric lines that stretched above the street. "We'll be watching for a yellow trolley that will travel along those lines up there, powered by electricity." She pointed to the trolley system that tied the city with the various neighborhoods by arteries of wires. Two large boom-type poles on the roof of the bus reached up to the over-the-street wires and powered the trollies.

Adam and Fritzy gazed with amazement at the well-structured system that connected the city both in a friendly way and, with the wires, in a literal way.

Then Adam stopped, his mouth gapping. "That's Mr. Weedy in the back of that Cadillac," he said as he pointed from the curb to the car that approached in the lane nearest them. "What kind of a job does he have? He lives in two rooms of a rooming house with only a hotplate to cook his food on and rides around town during work hours in a limousine."

"He's a scientific assistant at some company around town," Sunshine said slowly. It sounded to Adam like she was confused as well.

Adam continued to watch the car. "That's pretty good for government work."

The light turned red, and the fancy car had to stop right beside them. Mr. Weedy looked out of the side window, coming eye to eye with Adam, and then put his hand to his forehead as if he were shading his eyes from the sun. Adam was sure it was a gesture designed to conceal his face. Then the light changed to green.

As Adam watched, two dark shadows oozed out from the chrome grill on the front of the big car and slithered over the windshield to the top of the hood. Adam hadn't seen the evil shadows since he left Middletown, now here they were right out in the open. At least, there in the fresh air, their awful stench went undetected. In fact, no one seemed to notice them. *Why can't the driver see that the shadows are blocking his view?*

The answer came to Adam as the voice of Shaddi, the one who was always there, who spoke only of love. Adam's grandmother, Granny O'Hara, had warned against making eye contact with the shadows. She said, "They will seem to offer comfort, even healing, but they are evil. Once they have you, they will never let you go."

Adam couldn't shake loose of the mystery that was taking place in front of his eyes. Who were the Weedys and their associates? They brought out the evil shadows Granny O'Hara taught him to avoid. He wondered if Mr. Weedy was in trouble, or was he going to cause trouble?

Adam checked the license plate. It was a normal Ohio license with an emblem attached to the frame it was housed in. "Los Alamos Laboratory," Adam read. "What is Los Alamos Laboratory?"

"Never heard of it," Shine said as she gazed after the car as it moved on.

Fritzy offered a possibility. "Daddy said there is a secret facility out in New Mexico called Los Alamos."

"Has he been there?" Shine asked. "I've wondered what New Mexico would look like."

"A lot of sand and sunshine," Adam offered.

"You've been there?" Shine asked.

"No," he said. "I read a lot."

Fritzy shrugged. "No. My dad's never been there, but he's a Science teacher. I think he heard about it a couple of years ago at a conference of teachers. They were developing something called a Think Tank."

Adam shook his head. "So he heard of the New Mexico place at the Think Tank?" Adam couldn't believe it. He and Fritzy had been friends for a long time. "Why didn't you tell me that Coach had such an important job during the war?"

"Cause he didn't accept the invitation to participate," Fritzy said. "We would have had to move to New Mexico, and Daddy just had too many responsibilities in Indiana." Fritzy kept watching the tail end of the car that was, by then, several blocks down the street.

"Does any of this seem strange to either of you?" Adam leaned way over toward the road. He hoped to see the direction the vehicle would continue to travel.

"I guess I really don't know the Weedys very well after all," Sunshine admitted.

Fritzy wrinkled up her nose. "But, they live in your house," she protested.

Sunshine raised both hands up in surrender. "I didn't interview them for the apartment and I don't know what they told Momma and Daddy." She then reached in her pocket and pulled out some coins.

The cross town trolley pulled to a stop near the curb, and the driver opened the door. It could only get as close to the sidewalk as the electrically fed booms could reach. Adam and the girls hopped on.

The trolley smelled like soft pretzels someone had brought onboard and a few large salt pieces crunched under Adam's feet. He tried not to think about his stomach. After all, he ate a big breakfast not long before that. He took his seat and looked out the window. Trying to forget about Weedy and the classy car, he focused on the possibility of finding Sergeant Smith and eventually his missing father.

Chapter 11
The VA

The VA Hospital spread out before Adam as he, Fritzy and Shine got off the trolley. In the middle of the sprawling building, a tall white tower balanced the turrets on each side of the long edifice. There was a collective, "Wow," that escaped from all three.

"Where do we begin?" Fritzy asked.

Adam started off in the direction of the center of the building. "The front door I guess."   The long driveway that approached the Veterans' Hospital spanned the entire width of the structure. They entered through the center door.

"May I help you?" A rigid but pleasant enough woman, who sat at the information desk in the center of the hall, greeted the trio.

"We are looking for two people," Adam began and held his breath.

"Yes, young man. Who did you want to see?" Her round, black wire rimmed glasses with wrap-around-the-ear stems bobbed up and down on her nose when she spoke.

"Sergeant Smith and Will Shoemaker or Schumacher. William Schumacher," Adam concluded. Both of the girls looked at Adam with surprise written on their faces, but they said nothing.

The greeter ran her long fingernails down the list of patients, turned many pages until she rested on the S's. "Well, let me see," she mumbled. "Schumacher, William," she paused as she refined her search, "Schu…" Looking up at Adam, she smiled faintly. "I'm sorry, young man. We have no patient by the name of William Shoemaker or Schumacher."

"Well, okay," Adam sighed and wished he could talk to Shaddi. "It was a long shot. We haven't received official word about Pops." Adam's stomach flipped inside and turned sour. *Why is there a "no" at every turn?* He stretched over the high counter of the information desk and asked again about Sergeant Smith. Adam was sure there had to be something. "Smith isn't a patient. I think he works here."

"Oh, this isn't an employee directory," the receptionist tapped on the paper bound listing with her red fingernails. "It's a file of patients."

Adam grew impatient with the woman who held answers to his family's tragedy but didn't seem to care. He shoved his jittery hands into his pockets.

The woman reached under the desk and pulled out a small booklet with the word *Employees* printed out in large letters. Again, the long red nails scanned the pages. "Oh," she said slowly and looked up. "What color is he?"

"What color?" Adam asked and looked at Fritzy. His friend had ridden with him in Smith's car that day last winter when a snow storm came in while they were out at the Schumacher farm. Adam froze for a moment. With Smith showing up all the time, Adam had felt stalked. Color hadn't been an issue. Fear was all he thought about.

"Sergeant Smith is a man of very dark complexion," Fritzy over explained with attitude. "Does that matter? He is still the one who gave Adam a clue as to the whereabouts of his father. It wasn't a black clue. It was just a clue," Fritzy sassed.

"Well, no, it doesn't matter to me, young lady." The woman looked at Adam and his friends over her spectacles. "But, we have several workers here with the last name of Smith."

"Were they all Sergeants in the war?" Fritzy asked in a sugary sweet tone.

"Sergeant Smith?" the receptionist questioned as she looked through the directory again. She was silent as she searched, except for the heavy breathing of one who had lost interest in helping.

"Sergeant Smith," Adam repeated. It felt like this one, uncaring, unfeeling woman was all that stood between him and his father.

"Well, this may be...here is Captain Smith," Miss Indifferent said as she yawned. "He isn't working today. It's his day off." She closed the book and folded her hands.

"His day off?" Adam groaned and shook his head. "Not captain...sergeant," he repeated. *Shaddi,* he called inside his thoughts. *What now?* To the woman, he sighed and asked, "Can you give me his address or phone number?"

"Oh, my no," the receptionist bristled. "We're not permitted to give out personal information about patients or employees."

"You're kiddin'," Fritzy gasped. "We've come a long way." Then she asked with a sugary sweet tone, "Why do you call the Sergeant...Captain, or is it...you call the Captain... Sergeant?"

"We don't call *those* people by a rank they probably didn't even earn," she stiffened.

"*Those* people?" Fritzy asked.

"Well, never you mind," the receptionist refused to answer. "That's too bad that you've come so far, miss," the lady cooed as she unwound one stem of her glasses from her ear slowly and then the other. Obviously the topic of the sergeant, or captain, was over. "You will still have to come back tomorrow."

"Then, we will," Adam stately flatly.

Adam and the girls slumped out of the VA with deflated spirits. The spring air was intoxicating but they didn't seem to notice. They ignored the large beds of blossoming flowers in the center of the court yard as they stared only at the sidewalk under their feet.

"Tomorrow?" Adam moaned.

Fritzy poked Adam in the ribs impatiently. "It'll be okay, Schumacher." She paused a second. "Shine, do you think your parents would let us stay another night?"

Sunshine's expression changed from disappointment to possibilities. "I'm sure that's no problem. The eighth grade is on Easter break too, ya know—no homework, no early rising."

"I'll call Mom again," Fritzy said as they hurried along the sidewalk to the bus stop out front.

"Moms will understand," Adam said a little more rapidly, with hope in his voice. "She knows how important this is." Inside, he hoped another day would make the difference.

Chapter 12
Weedy's Front Room

"Don't let him get in the house," Grace Sullivan insisted as Sunshine opened the side door at the mid-floor landing on the way to the basement, or up to the kitchen. "Be careful to keep that brown squirrel outside on your way out." Then she paused and asked, "How did you happen to get up so early?"

"It isn't a school day. It's vacation." Shine smiled as she came out onto the side patio where her mother was re-potting one of her African violets. "That's pretty," she motioned toward the plant. "I like the purple ones better than the pink. Violet is not pink. Violet is a shade of purple, therefore an African violet should be a shade of purple."

"Very technical, dear," Grace stated patiently. "Is Fritzy up yet?" she asked. "I've been wanting to ask her about Aunt Arletta—how she's doing. Girls seem to know about these things more than boys."

Sunshine watched the squirrel scamper across the driveway. "Fritzy was putting her shoes on when I came out."

"And Mr. Schumacher?"

"Schumacher is here and accounted for," Adam reported with a salute as he came around the side of the house from the front porch glider.

"Sir," Mrs. Sullivan teased, "you had about two minutes in the shower on Sunday. Would you like to take a long, relaxing shower and change?"

"That would be great. I didn't want to get in the Weedys' way or your cousin and her family."

"I agree the bathroom is the busiest room in the house," Grace said as she dumped some fresh potting soil around the plant's roots. "We all share the one facility, but there is a very modest, single toilet in the basement for emergencies," she explained without stopping her potting project.

"There they are," Shine said as the Weedys stepped off the front porch and walked toward the garage.

"Well, he's all right this morning," Adam whispered.

"Oh course he's all right. What are you talking about?" Mrs. Sullivan waved at the couple and went back to the joy of re-planting her plant.

"Good morning," Adam greeted as they came closer. "How was that ride in the fancy car yesterday?"

"Don't know what you're talking about," Weedy snapped back.

"He was at work all day," his misses testified.

Sunshine put her hands on her hips and tossed her hair. "We saw you downtown in a fancy Cadillac. Sure looked like an expensive ride. We were on the curb and saw you riding in luxury."

"Shine! That's not polite." Grace Sullivan corrected. "We don't talk about the value or cost of someone's car—or any possession."

"Sorry," Sunshine answered but the set of her jaw indicated the apology was purely mechanical. "It wasn't his car. He was riding in the back."

"See you after work, Grace," Evelyn Weedy announced. She pulled on the Chevy door handle and quickly got in. Oliver put the car in gear and backed out.

To Adam's mind, the two were out of the garage and out of the driveway in record time. "Mrs. Sullivan, I know I saw Weedy in town yesterday, in the back of a Cadillac."

"If he can ride around town in a luxury car, why is he living in a rooming house?" Shine asked, following Weedy's car with her eyes, as it headed back up the street toward Wilmington Pike.

"Here, here," Grace cautioned her daughter. "You are quite the talker this morning. There is nothing wrong with living in a rooming house. The war was over less than a year ago. They can't build houses fast enough to meet all the needs. When we listed the apartment in the newspaper, cars lined up down the street and around the corner for a chance to get a few rooms in a clean house. And, I may add, this is our home, not a sleazy hotel."

"Sorry, Mama," Sunshine apologized. "Come on Adam," she quickly changed the subject. "Follow me and I'll get you a fresh towel so you can take that shower."

"Good morning," Fritzy greeted as she walked out of the house and stretched in the sun, adjusting her spine in the light.

"Morning." Adam walked right past her.

"Come on, Fritzy," Shine stepped up on the front steps, two at a time.

Fritzy spun around. "Where are we going?"

"Adam is going to take a shower. I'll get you a towel, too. Then you and I will have juice and toast while he hits the water. Then, it's your turn."

"A shower?" Fritzy threw her hands in the air and raced them to the front door, around the corner and up the steps.

Upstairs, there was an open hall with four doors that led to the four bedrooms in each corner of the house, an additional door to the one bathroom, and the door to a small linen closet.

"Hi Sunshine," Catherine Reynolds called from her sitting room in the northeast corner of the second floor where she sat crocheting.

"Good morning, Catherine," Sunshine said and walked over to the open door. "This is Adam Schumacher and Fritzy Breman. They're staying with us for a couple of days. If you're not going to be using the shower, they'd each like to use the bathroom," she announced.

"Say, Mrs.—"

"Catherine is fine, Adam," Grace's cousin said as she smiled.

"What ya know about the Weedys?" Adam asked.

"Oliver and Evelyn?" she paused in thought. "I guess not much. They come in late after work, close the door and I don't see them the rest of the night, except to slip into the bathroom late in the evening and early in the morning. Dave and I try to stay out of their way. They're both quiet."

"Secretive?" Adam asked.

"I hadn't thought about them keeping secrets," Catherine said slowly as she put her crochet work in her lap. "I don't know enough about them to know if something is a secret."

"Thanks Catherine. I'd better get these two some towels. Mom wouldn't want me to talk about people behind their back. I just didn't want you to freak out if you saw a strange man heading toward the shower." Shine took two towels from the small closet and pointed to the bathroom. "It's not big, but the water is hot."

"Not Big?" Adam laughed. "We had an outhouse on the farm. And, that was so little my knees nearly touched the wall when I sat down. Just before Pops left for the war, he had running water brought into the house and a small bathroom was installed under the steps in the first floor hallway."

"Adam!" Fritzy gasped. "We don't talk about bathrooms!"

"I know what you mean by tiny. That sounds like Grandma and Grandpa's farm before they moved into Greenville," Shine agreed with a knowing smile. "So, Adam, enjoy your shower," she said as she took Fritzy by the arm and led her back downstairs. "You'll have a lot more time under the water than you did yesterday."

Downstairs, Shine lead the way to the kitchen, through the living room and dining room. "There's some orange juice in a bottle in the refrigerator," she said. "If you'll get it out, I'll put some toast in." Shine lowered each side of the toaster, placed fresh bread on the wires and brought the sides up again.

Fritzy found the small Frigidaire in the kitchen and opened the door. A tiny freezing unit, about the size of a shoe box, hung in the middle at the top, at eye level. A quart of milk was on the right of the freezer and a bottle of orange juice on the left. "Got it," she called out in glee.

Once everything was ready, the girls took their breakfast into the dining room. Fritzy took a bite and said, "Does anything about all this sound strange to you?"

"About what?" Shine asked.

"I know, for sure, that was Weedy yesterday, unless he has a twin." Fritzy sipped at the orange juice and said no more.

Shine closed her eyes in thought. "I don't think there's a twin, but I don't know for sure. Maybe you saw a doppelgänger."

"A what?" Fritzy asked.

"A doppelgänger—someone who looks like someone else but isn't related to them," Shine said as she took a bite of toast.

Fritzy licked some melted butter from her fingers and asked, "Doesn't anybody know anything about the Weedys? That person we saw was no doppelgänger."

"Mr. Weedy works as a chemist at a company in town. Evelyn works for a patent attorney downtown. She's a research assistant or something." Sunshine went out into the kitchen and dropped two more pieces of toast as Adam came thudding down the stairs.

"Spotty," Adam reached over and petted the little black and white cocker-type dog. "She is either black with white patches or white with black patches, just like you said. Good morning." He looked her over again—"basically black," he concluded with certainty.

"My turn," Fritzy jumped up and darted past Adam on the way to the shower.

Adam sat down at the table, reached for his share of the toast, took a big bite and smiled when the warm butter began to drip from his chin. Sunshine pointed to the paper napkin under his elbow.

"We were just talking about the Weedys," she said. "But, we soon realized we don't have anything to talk about because we don't know much about them."

"Your folks sure trust people." Adam took another big bite of the toasted bread he had just slathered with Mrs. Sullivan's homemade Concord grape jelly.

"They do," Shine said and sipped her juice. "That's why they let you and Fritzy stay here."

"Ouch," he winced.

"Spotty," she reached down to the dog. "You are sure nervous this morning."

"She does seem jumpy," Adam agreed.

"That is so odd. Spotty is the calmest dog I've ever seen. I used to dress her up in doll clothes when I was little. I'd tell her to stay in my doll buggy until I came back. Then, I'd go off and play and forget all about her. When I'd come back, she'd be laying there under the buggy blanket with a bonnet on her head, taking a nap. She hadn't moved. This skittishness is not like her."

"Look at her," Adam pointed. The dog was wagging her whole hind half. "Now, she's faking a sneeze."

"That means she's mad," Shine explained with an exaggerated sigh and roll of her eyes. "She can be so dramatic."

The black and white bundle of fur darted into the living room, then back into the dining room. "Sneeze, sneeze, sneeze." Back into the front room and up two steps, then back to the table again.

"She wants us to follow her." Shine stood up, with Adam right behind her.

They walked up eight steps when Sunshine peered out the stair landing window. "Make sure the Weedys haven't come back for some reason. Mother wants us to stay off the second floor, except for baths and such."

The little dog ran up the steps and scratched at the Weedys' door. It was the other room in the front of the house, opposite the Reynolds' space. Spotty wiggled and twisted and sneezed at the closed door.

Sunshine peeked into Catherine's room. She was still crocheting in the chair beside the radio. Shine put her finger to her lips to caution Adam to maintain silence, and then eased the Weedys' doorknob. She held her breath and winched. Would the door to squeak?

Inside, the room was cozy and tidy. Newspapers, folded and placed in a small wooden magazine rack, were beside the desk. Spotty wiggled over to the front window and the bottom drawer of the desk.

"I've never seen that desk before," Shine mouthed.

"What about the other things in here?" Adam looked around the room at the soft, royal blue velvet couch and chair, and walnut end tables.

"Daddy bought everything through the Dayton Daily Newspaper classified ads," she continued in a whisper as she studied the new desk. "Everything we have is hand-me-down. Weedy must have moved the desk in when we weren't home, maybe during Sunday morning services or on a Sunday afternoon when we were with my grandparents."

They both looked at the locked lap drawer. "The lock probably secures all the drawers." Adam pulled gently on the center drawer and then tested the others down each side. "All locked."

Spotty sneezed again and butted the bottom drawer with her forehead. "She thinks she has antlers," Shine whispered. "That seems to be the only drawer she's interested in, so we'd better get out of here. Momma would be mad."

They silently backed out of the room and carefully pulled the door closed. When they heard Catherine turn down her radio and stand up, they slid onto the upper steps and sat down.

"Just waiting for Fritzy," Shine offered like there was absolutely nothing wrong when Catherine came out of her sitting room.

"Oh, I thought I heard a noise in the other apartment." She stepped into the hall and listened.

"We were whispering," Adam explained—an honest statement. "We didn't want to disturb your listening to the radio."

"Well, thank you for that." She stepped back into her setting room.

"Wow!" Fritzy said, and jumped as she stepped out of the bathroom. "How strange—a greeting party."

They laughed and buzzed as they went downstairs. Grace was sitting in front of the fireplace sipping a cup of coffee.

"What were you three up to?" She chuckled.

"We met Catherine," Fritzy offered—another honest statement.

Grace sat her cup on the side table and studied their faces. "So, what's happening today?"

"We're going to go back out to the VA and see if we can find Sergeant Smith. He may have a lead to my father." Adam sat on the edge of the sofa and tapped his fingertips together. He was anxious to get going.

Chapter 13
Sergeant Smith

"Same seats. Same three of us." Sunshine mused as she slid onto the bench seat along the back of the bus. The driver pulled away from the side of the road and began winding around, out of the neighborhood of Beavertown and through the streets of Oakwood, following the bus line just as they did the previous day as they headed toward the city.

"Now what?" Adam pointed out the window. "Look who's back—not at his laboratory, but in that same black car from yesterday."

The dark Cadillac turned off of Far Hills Avenue to the west, in the area of Oakwood. The man in the back seat was definitely Oliver Weedy. Adam jumped up and climbed with his knees onto the back bench beside Shine. He watched out of the rear window of the bus as two dark shadows rose up out of the pavement and stared at the long car and Oliver Weedy. They hissed, "He's mine...hiss." They jumped into the limo as the car turned and followed a bend in the road. The scene was soon far past the bus.

"Your Seedy Weedy leads quite a weed-infested life," Adam said as he settled back again. He dismissed the thought as quickly as he said it, but not so fast as to forget the dark ones who rode in the limo.

I am here, Shaddi whispered.

In the city, Shine jumped up and pulled the bell-rope that followed the curve above the side windows. The bus slowed to a stop. "Here," Shine announced. "We get off here."

They disembarked in front of the majestic old building with six huge columns out front they had seen the day before. "That's the Court House," Shine said as she pointed to the Ohio limestone building with its nine or ten graceful stone treads that rose up to an entry portico that spanned the entire front of the building. "Abraham Lincoln once stood on those steps and spoke to the people who had come just to hear him."

"How do you know all of that?" Fritzy stared at the massive building in awe.

The corners of Sunshine's mouth turned up ever so slightly as she cocked her head to the right. "I guess I just listen."

"To what?" Adam asked.

"I ride the bus all the time. People talk to those they're riding with and...I listen."

Adam closed his eyes and nodded. "I might try that," he agreed. Fritzy just shook her head in disbelief.

"Look," Shine pointed up East Third Street. "The cross town trolley is on time."

When the trolley stopped, the three quickly boarded and settled in for the trip down West Third Street. They sat in their previously staked-out seats and settled in for another trip through Dayton's streets.

Their ride was silent for the most part. Each seemed lost in their thoughts. Adam knew what was on his mind but he had trouble sorting it all out. There was Weedy's strange appearance in the back of a luxury car while he and his wife lived in two rooms with a shared bathroom. Mrs. Garver saw him walking along the railroad tracks. What is he, a depression era hobo on weekends, and one who drives a car to work during the week? A smelly dug-out where they found an out-of-place piece of paper that looked like the backing to a legal document. It was similar to the end sheet attached to the rental agreement for acreage the neighboring farmer signed with Pops before he went off to war. Wow, what a jumble of stuff.

Shine reached up and pulled the bell-rope. "We're here," she announced.

Adam, Fritzy and Sunshine got off at the corner and walked up the curved drive that led into the Veteran's Administration Hospital. The same lady that sat at the desk the day before was there again, with the same expression of indifference.

"May I help you?" she asked as she covered her mouth to stifle a yawned.

"We were here yesterday." Adam leaned on the reception desk.

"A lot of people go through here," she yawned again.

"We were looking for Sgt. Smith."

She opened the directory of patient names and scratched along the page with her long fingernails. "Don't see the name."

"You said yesterday that Smith is a worker here not a patient."

"Then why didn't you tell me that before I started looking?" She jerked the other book, the one with employees in it, from under the desk to a position in front of her and began to leaf through it.

"There is a Sgt. Smith who is an orderly in the orthopedic rehab department. Here is another Smith, social worker, in the department for those with sight problems."

Adam thought for a moment. "He sounds more like the social worker. He was trying to bring our family back together again." He rested one hand on the counter then the other. "Is he working today?"

"Yes, I'll call that department and see if I can find him." She picked up the receiver and dialed in four numbers. "Yes, thank you Margaret," she clack, clacked her nails on the desk, listened, and then spoke again. "I'm trying to reach Sgt. Smith. Is he around there right now?" She paused and listened for the response. "Does he have the time to come to the front lobby for a few minutes?" She listened again. "Thanks Margaret, you're the best." She listened again. "Catch me up on your date last night at lunch. Bye."

Adam waited as he shifted from his left foot to his right. Finally, he threw his arms in the air is surrender. "And?" he shrieked.

"He'll be right down," the receptionist sighed. She looked down at the desk and mumbled, "You young people need to learn to be more patient." Then she smiled a sickeningly sweet smile. "But, I'm very happy to help you."

"Your enthusiasm is appreciated," Fritzy said with a mocking smile.

The receptionist just yawned again, with her hand to her mouth.

The elevator doors swished open and the Blue-Car-man got off. He caught Adam's eye and his smile covered his face. "Mr. Schumacher," he reached out his hand. "It is so good to see you again."

"Schumacher?" Sunshine wrinkled up her nose in question. "How did he know your name?"

"It's a long story," Fritzy laughed. "Maybe he'll get around to telling it some other time."

"And, Miss Breman," the Sergeant extended his hand.

"Frederica," she offered her given name. "I don't think I thanked you for the ride back into town during that blizzard last Christmas."

"Yes, as I remember it, you did. But, you were very sleepy. And, your father thanked me, too." He motioned for the three of them to follow him over to an area of chairs. "Go ahead and sit down."

"I can't believe I found you," Adam sighed deeply. "I haven't found my father yet, Sergeant. Is he here in this hospital?"

"No Adam. He was...but, not anymore." His eyes lowered as he thumped his index finger on the armrest of the chair.

"Not anymore? You mean he was here all along?" Adam gasped.

"Several of the men who had amnesia were moved to a group home someplace here in town. I'll have to find out where and if you can see him there."

"He's right here in Dayton? I can't believe it." Adam ran his hand over his mouth as if he were trying to catch his breath. "If he's still here in town—that would be amazing."

"This may take some time, Adam. The psychiatrist said all the men in the group home are very fragile. Since they can't remember their name or their past they are blind men walking around, trying to find their way home."

"I guess I understand," Adam admitted. "I'm hoping that he'll remember me."

"Where can I reach you?" The Sergeant removed a piece of paper and a fountain pen from his shirt pocket.

"They're staying at our house for a couple of days," Sunshine explained. "We live in Beavertown, on Keystone Avenue. The phone number is Walnut 3332."

"I'll be in touch. It may take a couple of days." He started to reach out his hand, then stopped and embraced Adam. "We'll find him, son."

Chapter 14
The Evening

"This meatloaf is super, Mrs. Sullivan," Fritzy said as she blotted her mouth with her napkin.

The Sullivan family and their guests had gathered around the dining room table for supper at four PM as usual. That was the way it was for a post-war factory worker and his/her family.

"Mother makes the best meatloaf in Montgomery County," Sunshine beamed.

"Thank you. Appreciation is always nice. And, I thank you three for the batch of chocolate chip cookies you made. That will be a perfect dessert with a little bit of ice cream."

"You two should come more often if we're getting' cookies out of the deal." Dan Sullivan took out another helping of meatloaf and mashed potatoes.

"Jeepers, I can't thank you enough, Mr. Sullivan," Adam said with genuine appreciation. "I wouldn't have been able to look for my father if I didn't have a place to stay. You and Mrs. Sullivan made that possible."

"You'll have to thank Aunt Arletta, too. When she and Uncle Alfred asked if it would be all right for you to stay here, I said sure."

"I'm sorry you didn't know Adam wouldn't be alone—there would be two of us. I was the eager beaver and snuck into the back of the truck." Fritzy picked up her glass of milk and held it in front of her face. Embarrassed, she hid behind her glass.

"You are a delight, young lady." Grace threw her head back and chuckled.

"Arf, arf, arf, arf," Spotty came shrieking and barking down the steps.

"I do apologize," Oliver Weedy said, following the dog, matching her step for step. "She snuck into my room right behind me. I didn't see her. When she tried to root through my desk drawer, I shooed her away. She may have gotten knocked down." His words sounded sincere.

The three looked at each other, but no one said anything. Their eyes were round and wide. Adam was suspicious. *That's what Spotty had her tail in a kink about this morning—something about the desk.*

"You put in a desk up there?" Dan asked.

"Yes…I…ah…hope that's all right." Weedy stammered.

"All right? Of course. I just didn't see ya move one in. I'd of helped ya." Dan sipped his coffee.

"I guess it was a Sunday morning some months back," Weedy admitted carefully.

"Really," Sullivan added. "What store? There ain't none open on a Sunday?"

"Oh," he stammered, "I don't remember."

"We'll try to keep the dog down here," Grace offered.

• • •

"Our favorite radio show, Fibber McGee and Molly, will be on in a few minutes," Grace said as she adjusted the floor standing Philco radio's tuning dial and sat down in a comfortable chair.

Adam started to sit down on the couch but Sunshine stopped him. "Daddy always lies down on the couch in the evening."

"I can hear the stories about Wistful Vista right here on the floor," Adam said as he sat near the fireplace and radio.

"Me too," Fritzy agreed and parked herself beside him on the old Persian carpet.

"I have canasta cards, if you want to play while we listen," Shine said as she got the deck out of one of the windowed bookcases that flanked the fireplace.

"This's nice," Adam said, looking around the warm room full of fun people. He watched Dan Sullivan lie down on the sofa and throw one leg over the back. "When Pops was home, he usually slept on the couch in the evening, too." His words drifted off as he remembered all he had lost when the War Department drafted his pops. He was gone for three years and counting. His unit had come home when the war was over the previous June. Pops hadn't.

"You'll find him," Fritzy encouraged him. She had known Adam for years, and she knew what he had been through. She had also been with him when Sergeant Smith came to town looking for the Schumacher family. He had Will Schumacher's dog tags.

"It finally feels like I just might," Adam agreed.

Shine unboxed the double-decked canasta cards, one-hundred eight cards in all. She shuffled one deck at a time, then the two decks together and dealt eleven cards to each player. The game began just as Fibber McGee opened his closet door and everything fell out, with a bang and a clatter–an event that happened in every radio performance. Everyone laughed and settled in for the evening.

An animal shriek filled the room and drowned out the audience's laughter coming from the radio.

"What on earth?" Grace jumped. Her Good Housekeeping magazine flew in the air.

Spotty squealed in pain, barked and flew down the stairs. Sneeze, sneeze, wiggle, wiggle—she did her *follow-me-and-scold-someone* dance.

"I didn't even see her sneak back upstairs again," Adam said.

No one came downstairs with an explanation for the dog's terror. There was no sound above but the slamming of a door.

"What the…was that all about?" Dan sat up, startled and confused.

"I have no idea." Grace shook her head in disbelief. "She hasn't acted like that since the neighbor down the street accidently hit her as he passed by in his car. She came sneezing to me so I would go down there and bawl him out."

"So, she's basically tattling on someone when she acts like that?" Adam watched the dog continue her angry little antics.

"Are you going to go up there and find out what happened?" Shine asked her dad.

"No, not this time." Dan settled back down. "The dog isn't s'pposed to be up there." He stated flatly. "The Weedys pay rent. Spotty don't."

"How much would she have to pay?" Fritzy asked in fun.

"Well, now lemme see," Dan began with a twinkle in his eye. "Her room is the basement landing. That's a space about three feet by three feet. Pretty small sleepin' room. But, then she does get room *and* board. So her food would figure into that monthly bill. Maybe, two dollars a week? How does that sound?"

"Sounds fair to me, Mr. Sullivan," Adam joked. All in all, it was a good evening.

Chapter 15
Finding Mrs. Henry

"Spotty," Grace called from the back door. "Where is that dog?" she muttered as she walked outside, across the drive, then around and up the front steps.

"I haven't seen her," Sunshine said as she followed her mother out into the fresh morning air. The cherry trees on the other side of the yard were blooming full and sweet, with the hint of cherry pie in the future.

"I've been out here on the porch all morning," Adam said as the two joined him. "I guess I haven't seen Spotty either, come to think of it."

Grace shook her head and turned toward the empty acre beside the yard. "She's probably out in the field gathering burrs in her fur. Never mind the dog. What's on your agenda for today?" Grace asked as she sat down on one of the porch chairs that flanked the glider.

"I don't have any idea," Adam admitted. "We're waiting for Sergeant Smith to call. I don't want to get too far away from the phone. But, I'll go batty if we just sit here."

"I can take a message for you if you three want to go someplace," Grace offered. "Sunshine checks in from time to time. I'll give her a few more nickels. She can call in hourly."

"Maybe we can look for Spotty," Fritzy offered.

"Okay," Adam jumped up and started down the front steps.

The three headed toward the garage whistling for the dog all the way. "Spotty," they called in every corner of the large old carriage house. Nothing. They walked around the side of the large barn-shaped building to where the grape arbor behind the garage was just beginning to leaf out and show the promise of fruit.

"Don't reach into the arbor. There's usually a snake in there," Shine warned. "But, go ahead and grab her if you see a dog hanging from the vines." They walked past the tall swing Dan had made from long galvanized pipes and secured with elbow joints, and on through the opening in the fence at the back of the garden. Along the right side of the property line lilac bushes had already started to bloom and sent the unmistakable aroma of fragrant lavender into the air.

"Doesn't look like your parents do much gardening." Adam looked around the overgrown garden that had obviously not produced a vegetable in several years.

"When we first moved out here from town," Sunshine giggled, "Daddy dug up this entire area behind the garage for a garden. Then, he walked off with the assumption that Momma would work the ground more finely, plant the seeds, do all the weeding, harvest the vegetables and do the canning. Mother simply said, 'No, thank you.' And, that was the last time he plowed the ground for a garden. It hasn't grown a blade of grass since then."

"Sorry, Sunshine." Fritzy put her hands on her hips and looked over the weeds. "The grass doesn't stand as tall as the dog. If she were hiding in here we would certainly see her."

Shine wrinkled up her hose. "I know. Now, I'm getting worried."

"Does she ever go downstairs," Adam asked, "into the basement?"

"Only if Mom is down there doing the laundry. Spotty keeps her company," Sunshine sighed. "But, let's go down and check it out. She might have accidentally gotten closed off in the fruit room."

They went into the house through the side door at the landing and then on downstairs. The basement smelled a little musty but there wasn't the stench of the dark shadows down there. So, Adam wasn't worried about the basement holding secrets no one wanted to discover.

Shine opened the coal room door and peered in. Over her shoulder, Adam couldn't see anything but blackened walls and the remaining shovels-full of black carbon rocks. It appeared to be just enough coal for a few cold spring nights—nothing else.

The fruit-room door was covered in a black fabric to help hold in the coolness that existed in the room located under the front porch. The room held newspaper lined shelves along the right where canning jars, that looked to Adam to be the last harvest of peaches and some jars of cherries, stood side by side. The room smelled both musty and fruity. The last of a bushel sack of yellow delicious apples still sat on the floor—but, no dog.

"Does Spotty ever run off?" Fritzy asked.

"Not like she doesn't come back. Most of the time, though, she stays in the yard. But, since she's not in the yard, let's go look." Sunshine started up the basement stairs and back out into the warm spring day. Next to the side yard, in the open field, there were tall grasses with a scattering of small milkweed pods in the marshy spots.

"I have on clodhoppers." Adam looked out across the open space. "I'll be happy to walk through the field and look for the dog if you want me to."

"I don't think so," Shine said slowly. "She wanders into the field and gets burrs in her coat, but, if I call her, she comes." Her voice sounded hopeful yet hesitant. It was obvious to Adam that Shine was getting more worried with each place they searched and found nothing.

Then they took to the street and followed it down to where it dead ended past the field. "Who lives here?" Fritzy asked as they approached a tiny green cottage next to the field. It looked run down and spooky.

"Mrs. Henry," Shine said as she followed the overgrown sidewalk and stepped up onto the worn wooden porch. "Her house is in shambles because she is so old and can't take care of it. But, she's a very nice lady. Mostly, she sits in her chair in the living room and listens to the radio. She's nearly blind."

As they reached for the door knob, black shadows rose up out from between the porch floor boards and sent their unholy scent into the air.

"What is that smell?" Fritzy asked.

"I'm sorry. Her place does stink," Shine apologized. "I don't know if she even gets a bath very often. It's very sad. She was a nurse during WWI and here in the United States when she got back. She would be mortified if she could actually smell things now."

"She lives all alone?" Adam peered in through the dirty front window.

We will help you find the dog, the shadows oozed out sounds only Adam could hear. *Just depend on us.*

"No," Adam stated sharply.

"No, what?" Shine asked.

"Don't ask," Fritzy said. "Adam answers questions that haven't been asked."

Shine knocked on Mrs. Henry's door. There was no response. Then Adam knocked, a little harder. The door pushed open. When it opened so easily, they looked at each other in surprise. All three stiffened their bodies and pinched deep furrows in their brows. Very slowly, Adam opened the door completely, and gasped.

Mrs. Henry was slumped forward in her chair. The smell in the room was enough to produce immediate gags from all of them. All three stood frozen just inside the doorway, their senses, paralyzed by the foul odor, refused to enter further.

"Oh no," Shine whispered. "I can't—." She did not step closer.

"I'll check her," Adam offered. He walked slowly to the woman in the chair and reached for her wrist. Picking up her limp right hand, he felt for her pulse. "Nothing."

We saw it all, the shadows belched as they breathed heavy foul air into the room.

As Adam placed the old woman's hand back on the arm rest, her body slumped forward. He jumped back as they all gasped in horror. The back of Mrs. Henry's head, covered in blood, gapped open.

They stared at each other, frozen. What if someone else was in the house? Someone who had harmed the woman? They hurried out the door, down one step off the porch and ran all the way to the Sullivans' house.

Up the street, turn into drive; up one, two, three, space, one, two, three more steps. The porch, the door— "Mom!" Sunshine yelled.

"Gracious, what on earth is wrong?" Grace came in from the kitchen drying her hands on a tea towel.

Instantly, words spilled out all over the floor. "She's dead!"

"The back of her head is all covered in blood, Mrs. Sullivan!" Adam was out of breath and panting, not from running, but from fear.

"Who?"

"Mrs. Henry!" Fritzy yelled.

"Oh, dear me. The poor woman," Grace put her hand to her chest and patted it, soothing the child within.

"Do I call the police or an ambulance?" Grace talked to herself as she headed toward the telephone that sat at the bottom of the staircase.

"The police, I think Mrs. Sullivan" Adam suggested. "I felt for her pulse and there was nothing there. But, the clincher was, I'm sorry girls," he said turning back to Fritzy and Shine, "the back of Mrs. Henry's head was gone."

"You children had to discover this on your own?" Grace gasped. "That is awful. I am so sorry. I should never have sent you looking for the dog." She took a handkerchief from her pocket and wiped her eyes. With trembling hands she picked up the receiver and paused. "I don't know what the police department number is," she said weakly.

"I'll check the telephone book, Momma," Shine said as she ran to pick up the thick book that sat under the telephone. Her hands were shaking so badly it was hard to turn the pages but there in the front was a list of emergency numbers. "Here it is, Walnut 6446."

No one sat down. They each paced in a parallel pattern and then all gathered around the telephone. Every moment was heavy with fear and sadness.

"Hello? This is Grace Sullivan on Keystone Avenue here in Beavertown. The little old lady who lives next door is dead."

She looked at the children around her and closed her eyes. "We think she's been murdered."

Chapter 16
Officer Gilbert

Adam, the girls and Grace sat on the front porch in silence, each alone in their own thoughts.

Suddenly, Grace whispered, "I just can't shake the life-changing image of you three young people finding a dead body."

Fritzy and Sunshine nodded. Adam too couldn't chase the grizzly picture of Mrs. Henry from his mind.

Finally, in the distance, they heard the plaintive wail of a police siren. They looked at one another but said nothing. When the car turned off Wilmington Pike onto Harvest Avenue, the four walked out to the edge of the driveway and waited. The police car pulled up beside them and Grace stepped up to the car window to speak to the officers.

"I'm Officer Gilbert, Ma'am," he introduced himself. "And, this is Officer Young, my partner."

"Yes, sir," Grace said quickly. "The children found her," she offered. "This is Adam Schumacher and Fritzy Breman. They're from Indiana—visiting for a few days."

"Okay," the officer acknowledged the two.

Then Grace continued. "Adam tested for a pulse and found none. Then when she slumped over, it was easy to see she was gone."

"Can any of you tell me more about it?" The officer asked. He pulled into the driveway and stepped out of the car.

Adam cleared his throat and squared his shoulders as he faced the officer. He remembered that Pops had always told him to look people in the eye when you were talking to them. "We were looking for Sunshine's dog. We had checked all around the house and in the basement, behind the garage and in the garden, but she wasn't here." He looked over at Fritzy and remembered all their adventures at home. This was much bigger. "We started down the street, checking the empty field as we passed. We came to Mrs. Henry's house and called around her yard for the dog. Then we went up on the porch and knocked on the door." Adam paused and tried desperately to catch his breath. He coughed and cleared his throat.

"When the lady didn't answer, we knocked again. This time the door easily pushed open. We could see her sitting in her chair, slumped over." His body shuddered involuntarily as he thought about the odor that overtook them all. "I volunteered to check her pulse. Since I'm not from Beavertown and didn't know her, I thought it was better that I check. When I replaced her hand on the arm rest of her chair, she fell forward. We could see the back of her head covered in blood." Adam blocked a gag reflex as best he could. "We came back here to the house, told Mrs. Sullivan, and she called you right away." Adam put his hands to his mouth then quickly slammed them both into his pockets. He had repeated all that he knew.

"Do you mind accompanying me back to her house again, son? You can describe what you had seen again as I look over the room."

"Sure," Adam agreed but his shoulders tightened.

The officer left the squad car parked at the end of the driveway.

"I'm going, with you," Fritzy announced.

"Me, too," Sunshine chimed in. She trailed behind them for only a second but soon caught up.

The policeman and his partner hurried down toward the little house. As they got closer, the officer put out his hand and motioned for everyone to slow down. Moving his hand to his revolver, he approached the porch slowly. At the door, he pushed it open and stopped. The scene was the same as the three had described. Mrs. Henry, slumped over in her chair, didn't move. Dried blood pooled on her shoulder and down her body.

"You three were right," Officer Gilbert said as he touched the body, felt for her pulse, and looked over the scene. "I suppose she could have fallen, hit her head, and then sat down in the chair to steady herself. But, she was very old. I doubt that she would've had the energy to get back up off the floor from where she fell with that kind of injury." He looked around and then added. "You guys stay on the porch and wait for me there." The three watched through the open door but stayed out of the way.

Gilbert walked into the bedroom and checked the floor and furniture. "No signs of blood," he said to Young. Then, they went into the kitchen and tiny bathroom. "If someone has been here, they're gone now." Back in the sitting room, with furniture worn slick to the touch, the two men had to step aside to let the other wiggle past. Gilbert inspected the back of Mrs. Henry's head without touching her. "It looks like a gunshot wound."

"I agree," Young added. "You can see where it entered the back of her skull."

"The kids didn't see the entry point. What fooled them at first was, there is no exit wound," Gilbert whispered to Young.

Another siren approached in the distance. "That'll be the ambulance," Officer Gilbert said as he stopped and listened. "It'll be here in a few minutes. Is there anything else that you can remember that you haven't told me?" he asked the three as he stood in the open door.

Adam and the girls looked at each other and shrugged. Their posture wilted as their confidence ebbed away.

Sunshine explained. "The reason we came down here in the first place is because my dog is missing and we looked everyplace else and couldn't find her." As she stared in through the doorway, her eyes seemed fixed on the body of Mrs. Henry.

"I can't see how the dog would have anything to do with this murder." The policeman looked out the window toward Wilmington Pike.

"Spotty hardly ever came down here. Most of the time she stayed around home." Shine's eyes didn't shift—neither right nor left.

The officer looked again toward the back door and the backyard. Right in front of the door he stooped and picked up something. "Do you recognize this?"

All three gasped. The three knew what it was. It was a dog collar, and Sunshine knew which dog it belonged to.

"That's Spotty's." Tears came into Shine's eyes and she wiped her nose on the back of her hand.

"Was it broken before, Sunshine?" Adam looked at the collar. But then, it didn't look broken. It looked torn in two. "What is going on around here?" he asked. "I don't even have to leave Mrs. Henry's house to know that things are out of kilter."

Gilbert studied Adam intently. "So, is there anything else that you're basing your thoughts on? Did anything else happen I need to know about?"

"Two strange things happened." Adam looked first at Shine and then at Fritzy. "I don't know how common it is, Sunshine, but it sure seems strange to me."

"That's right, Adam," Shine said as her eyes opened wide. "Spotty acted angry sometimes before, but this time it seemed related, like it's all adding up to something."

They looked up the street as the ambulance turned off the highway and headed toward them. "Last evening," Shine explained, "we heard Spotty squeal in pain from upstairs. She came charging downstairs while we were in the dining room eating supper with Momma and Daddy. She came in wiggling and sneezing like she always does when she wants us to follow her. When she gets mad at somebody, she wants us to come and punish them."

"Then yesterday morning," Shine continued, "Spotty sputtered and carried on again so we followed her upstairs. She wanted to get into the Weedys' apartment. We're not allowed to go into the apartments, but I realized that something was going on." She didn't look at the officer. She kept her eyes away from him when she talked about something that would have gotten her in trouble with her mother.

"It wasn't all her. I went in with her," Adam admitted.

Sure, the shadows mocked. *Get into trouble. You don't have to tell anyone. Just lie about it. The police will never know.*

Adam ignored the evil ones. "Up in Weedy's sitting room, Spotty went over to the desk and wanted to get into the bottom drawer, but it was locked."

"You tried the drawer?" Officer Young asked.

"Yes, I'll have to admit we did," Fritzy chimed in.

"Then, did the dog calm down?" Gilbert put his hand on Adam's shoulder.

"Not really, I guess," Adam said. "But we got distracted. We heard Shine's cousin get up from her needle work in the next room and we got out of there."

The officer looked at the three of them with a little smile on his lips. "Sounds like you guys were smart. I usually get out of places I'm not supposed to get into right before I get caught, too."

The three looked at each other and exhaled in unison.

"So, the dog must have come down here for some reason." Gilbert walked around a little, still looking at the floor, searching for anything. "Then, we don't know what happened. But, Mrs. Henry was killed, the dog's collar was torn off and now the dog is missing."

The ambulance pulled up in front of the house. The driver and assistant got out, ran around to the back of the vehicle, opened the double doors and pulled out the gurney.

Adam had memories of the day Mr. Gunderman collapsed in his arms at the church. The ambulance came and took him away, too. But, he got better. Mrs. Henry was gone by the time they found her. She wouldn't be coming home.

"No need to hurry, men," the Officer said to the responders. "She's gone."

"That's part of the protocol. We don't deviate from our plan." The driver reached for the woman's wrist and took her pulse again. He wrote something on a piece of paper. Next, he felt the skin on her arms, her cheeks and her forehead. He wrote something else on the paper. Then, he motioned to the other worker. Together, they lifted her gently to the gurney and rolled her out of the house.

"After the autopsy, we may have a few other questions, but I don't really anticipate any." Gilbert patted Adam on the shoulder and smiled at the girls. "I need you two to stay around for another day while we try to sort things out. Then, if you will leave your home address and telephone number, I would appreciate it."

"Fritzy and I will have to leave if we get word about my father."

"Your father?"

"He's been missing. I think, the last anyone saw him the enemy captured him at the Battle of the Bulge. A Sergeant is trying to get information about him for me. It's been so long, sir. If he calls, I want to be able to go." Adam watched the man and hoped the officer was listening to him, his words and his emotions.

"We'll see, son. We'll see. Right now, if a patrol car drives by, that truck of yours had better be parked in the Sullivan's driveway."

"Yes, sir," Adam agreed but inside, his heart dropped to his laced up boots. How was he going to find Pops if he couldn't leave the Sullivan house?

Chapter 17
The Two Followers

"What on earth did ol' Schumacher get himself into?" Buddy Phillips questioned aloud, with a special emphasis on the German pronunciation of Adam's name, as he studied the whole scene from the corner up on Harvest Avenue.

Freddy Alexander smirked with his usual lopsided smile. "A crooked smile for a sleazy crook," Adam would have said. Freddy shook his head. "I can't believe that guy has gotten in trouble with the law. And him, the biggest boy scout in Middletown."

"What do you think he did?" Buddy asked as he leaned forward and rested his arms on the steering wheel of his old beat up rust-bucket.

As another police car went past, Freddy slumped farther down in the seat. From his vantage point, he could barely see through the windshield. "We followed the hero of Middletown High School all the way to this little suburb. Why? This ain't the beach or the mountains. It's no-where USA, Buddy."

Buddy anxiously tapped his fingers on the wooden steering wheel. "I wanted to watch his face when he realizes he lost his precious Sergeant-paper."

Freddy yawned and burped. "What ya mean 'watch' Buddy-boy? We can't even see him from here?" He doubled up his fist and pounded his chest. "We slept in the car, and I got cramps in my legs. All for this big-man-at-school? Let's go, I'm hungry."

"I saw a little diner up there on Wilmington Pike," Buddy said as his stomach growled, too. "But, how are we going to keep him in our sights?"

"Well," Freddy yawned again, "we can watch his truck. If that big farm clunker is still filling up that driveway, Schumacher won't be far away."

"Mom gave me some money," Buddy said as he fished in his jeans pocket. "You'd better have your own."

Freddy sat up a little taller. "Don't you worry about me. I always have money."

"Yeah," Buddy blistered back. "Yours or some bucks you lifted off somebody else?"

"Hey," Freddy shot back. "It wasn't my idea to steal that Christ Child carving last Christmas. That was all you."

"That's not how I remember it," Buddy growled.

"You always twist your memory to make the story come out to your advantage."

"I remember things as they happened, not how I want them to be," Buddy bellowed as the veins in his neck bulged.

"You just think if you yell loud enough everyone will agree with you," Freddy sniped back.

"If you really want me to yell," Buddy hissed out as his volume elevated again, "I can shout with the best of them."

"Loud doesn't make right," Freddy said as he folded his arms across his chest and slunk down again in the passenger seat.

"We'll go find some doughnuts or something," Buddy relented. "Maybe you'll be a little more agreeable."

"Me?" Freddy gasped. "I'm not the demanding, grumpy one."

"Oh, shut up, Freddy," Buddy grumbled as he put the car in gear and turned around. "You might as well give up. You know I'll win." He turned the car around, headed back up to the highway and turned left toward the little shops in Beavertown.

Chapter 18
Get Out and Get Movin'

Back in the Sullivans' living room, all three plus Grace, sat around staring at the floor. "You three have been through a real scare," Grace sympathized with her daughter and their new friends. "Why don't you all get out and do something to take your minds off of it?"

"What?" Sunshine took off her glasses and twirled them in her fingers.

"Well, you could go skating or go to a movie. Oh, there's a new exhibit at the Dayton Art Institute." Grace stopped and watched the three. "Maybe you three could think of something."

"I don't know," Fritzy whispered.

"I just hate it that you have been exposed to this terrible crime," Grace whispered.

"Yes Ma'am. It's not your fault. But—" Adam soothed as he watched Mrs. Sullivan wipe tears from her eyes. "Girls, I think Shine's mom would feel better if we had fun someplace." Then he stopped and scratched his head. "How are we going to do that if I can't leave town or move the truck?"

"Yes," Grace agreed with a nod through her tears. "Adam is right. I would feel better."

"What about a movie?" Sunshine asked. "I love movies. I think there's a good one at Keith's Theater, downtown," she offered.

"It will be my treat," Grace offered. "Sunshine, please bring me my purse from the closet."

"Thank you, Mrs. Sullivan," Adam said.

Sunshine opened the mirrored door of the closet at the foot of the stairs and got her mother's purse from the shelf above winter coats and spring sweaters, and handed it to her. "Here, Momma," she offered. "We'll be going to a matinee so—at thirty-four cents apiece, that would be a dollar and two cents."

"Okay," Grace said as she handed Shine the cash. "Here's money for the movie, bus fair and a small bag of popcorn each."

"Thanks," Adam and Fritzy said together.

Shine shoved the money into her pocket as the three started toward the door. "We don't need the truck, Adam," she said again. "We'll take the bus and get off a half-block from the theater on Fourth Street." Then she added, "I'll call you, Mom, and let you know where we are."

•••

Once again, Adam and the girls left the house and walked out into the beautiful spring day complete with a blue sky and bird songs from the treetops. No one would have guessed that the three had discovered a terrible tragedy just a little while before.

"Hi, Sunshine," Mrs. Ladderbach called from her comfortable spot on the porch swing across the street.

"Hi, Mrs. Ladderbach," Shine said as she waved.

Adam, Fritz and Shine walked up to the stop just in time to meet the next in-bound bus, boarded and took their usual seats.

•••

The two card-carrying members of the lazy-boys club arrived on the corner just minutes after the bus pulled into the south-bound lane and moved on down the street, to circle around before going north. Buddy rounded the bend onto Harvest Avenue and pulled to a stop by the side of the road.

"I can still see the Diamond T parked in that driveway," Freddy said as he stretched up tall enough to observe the Sullivan home. "So...our plan is to just sit here until it moves?"

"That's it," Buddy said as he leaned on the steering wheel again.

"How boring is that?" Freddy grumbled.

"We can take turns closing our eyes," Buddy offered. "Maybe even nap."

"I can sure use a nap," Freddy admitted.

"You can sleep your life away, Freddy," Buddy said as he shook his head.

"Yup," he agreed. "Sounds good to me." Freddy closed his eyes and quickly snorted out some nasty sounds. Buddy just rolled his eyes.

Chapter 19
Runnymede

"This whole thing seems so disconnected," Adam whispered as he settled onto the center-facing seat at the back of the bus. "Spotty's response to something in the desk up in Weedy's front room; the fresh piece of blue legal paper we found in the dug-out; and now the death of Mrs. Henry. And yet, it seems like it's all connected somehow. We just don't know in what way. How is that possible?"

"I know what you mean," Fritzy agreed.

Adam watched Beavertown pass by outside the bus. Clean, recently built brick homes for returning veterans and their longed for families lined whole stretches along the side of the road. It was nothing like Middletown where each house was the same as always, white frame with wide porches, all lined up in a row up and down the street. "I can see some kind of connection running to everything but I can't find a reason why."

"These houses remind me of all the new ones they're putting up on the north side of Middletown, near Johnson's Woods," Fritzy said.

"What are you talking about?" Adam snapped at the interruption of his thoughts.

Fritzy's mouth dropped open as she spoke. "Adam, I'm talking about the whole cluster of pretty little houses that are being built north of the high school back home."

Adam stared at her for a minute and then blinked. "I didn't know they were building homes up there."

Fritzy's disbelief softened to empathy. "Adam, you have been going to school, taking care of your mom, working at the church, planning the planting at the farm and making plans to come over here to Dayton to look for your dad. I doubt if you have even been north of the school in months."

"No," Adam whispered, his gaze fixed outside of himself and the bus again. "No, I hadn't heard about the new construction."

They all said nothing for several miles. Each seemed far off, within themselves, their eyes fixed on the passing scenery. Suddenly, Adam's eyes bulged with excitement. He jumped up, nearly falling over his own feet, and pulled the cable above the seats to signal for the driver to stop.

"This isn't a stop, kid." The driver called back over his shoulder and continued down the street.

"I know," Adam said and motioned for the others to follow him as he walked to the side door of the bus. His eyes, still focused on something he had seen outside, never checked to see if the girls followed. His gaze, fixed like stone on something neither of the other two seemed to notice, was so rigid it left no attention for the actions of others.

"Hang on," the driver said with a gruff sigh to his voice. He continued up another block and a half then pulled the long bus to the curb. The driver pulled the hand lever to the side to open the door and the three got off.

"Adam, what's going on?" Shine asked several times as she looked around. "We won't have money for bus fare to get back home from here."

"Sure we will," Adam said. "If that dog I just saw in the back of a car was Spotty, and I'm sure it was, we can't take her into a movie theater. So, we'll have our movie money to get back to Beavertown again."

"We're in the Oakwood area," Shine explained. "What on earth would my little dog be doing here?"

Adam could understand what Shine was talking about. It was a fancy neighborhood. But, he knew that he knew what he saw.

Large elegant houses lined both sides of the street. Graceful trees added to the picture with newly budding leaves the pale green of spring. The neighborhood was beautiful with its manicured shrubs and budding flower beds. It was all amazing and nothing at all like Middletown, Indiana. Adam smiled. As closely as he looked, he couldn't see vegetable gardens or tall sunflowers like the ones near the barn on the farm.

"Why did we get off?" Fritzy asked again.

"This sounds strange, but I know I saw Spotty. And, you want to hear something even stranger? She was sniffing at the air through the partially open back window of that same Cadillac we saw Seedy Weedy in."

"What?" Shine gasped. "That would be wonderful, Adam; but, you have to be seeing things. We've all been through a lot and it's starting to get to you," Shine shrugged and rolled her eyes. "This is Oakwood...it's like a small Hollywood. Do you think Rita Hayworth would have a little mutt like Spotty as her pet?"

Trust your own eyes, Shaddi whispered to Adam's heart.

"No...but, I know what I saw." He pointed down a side street. "Down there. The car carrying Spotty turned that way." He started walking and the girls followed. At the corner of Runnymede Road and Dixon Avenue they stopped.

"That's the Runnymede Playhouse," Sunshine nearly choked, her eyes open wide. "It used to be a place to play, just like the name says," she said as she squinted toward the end of the block. "There was a ballroom, indoor squash and tennis courts and even a stage for local productions." She wrinkled up her nose in confusion. "It's owned by a very wealthy family in town. Now look at it," she pointed. "It's guarded by men in uniforms, like a fortified castle."

"Good grief," Fritzy sighed. "Everything is so confusing."

Shine stared at the entire grounds. "Daddy took us past the Playhouse one day when we were out for a drive. It didn't look anything like this. In fact, when I first saw it, women in summer dresses and white gloves were giggling as they went up to the door. Now, a high fence protects the place with guards at the gate. Oh," she gasped again and jumped out of the way as two big trucks lined up at the gate to pass inspection and enter the facility. Shine brushed flying dust that flew up from the huge tires, from her pedal-pushers. "Besides, what on earth would they want with a mixed breed little dog, when they could buy as many pedigreed pups as they would want?"

"I have no idea what's going on." Adam looked neither right nor left but kept going. "I don't know why. I don't know how. I don't know who. I only know that Spotty was in that black Cadillac limousine." He looked at Shine. "You might say I had a gut feeling."

"If Adam says he had a feeling," Fritzy said as she took his arm. "He had a feeling."

"You know I want you to be right, Adam," Sunshine shook her head. "I'm torn between wanting it to be Spotty so badly I can pop...and doubt that it could be possible." She paused and studied the gate and guards. "Look, could the guards at the end of the driveway mean there is some great Hollywood star at the Playhouse today, maybe for lunch, to have that much protection around them."

"Lunch?" Fritzy choked a giggle. "It takes twenty or thirty armed guards to protect a fuzzy-headed actress while she eats salad and drinks mint julep?" She put her hand to her eyebrows and tried to block the sun from shining in her eyes.

"You're not that far south, Fritzy," Shine cracked. "You have to get to Cincinnati and cross the bridge before you get to the mint juleps of Kentucky Derby fame."

"Let's get back to why we're here," Adam insisted and rolled his eyes. Under his breath, he breathed out, *Girls.* "Somehow, we have to get in there, past all those guards, and not be seen."

"Adam," Fritzy began in protest, "those guards have guns—big, long barreled guns." She folded her arms and lowered her head in a perfectly executed pout.

"I see that," he snapped back. "I don't want us to walk past the front of the building and through the main gate. We don't have any reason to be here. We wouldn't get in and we'd be on display for everyone inside to see." Adam surveyed the layout of the estate. Then, he pointed out a possible plan. "Let's see if we can walk through the neighbor's yard on the right side. Then we can make a wide circular approach to the backyard of the Playhouse estate. I don't know if they'll see us. I don't know what's in the back of the building; but, that's the only idea I have."

Fritzy's fists grew tight. "Wait a minute, Adam. Let's talk about this," she cautioned.

"Wait?" he whispered hoarsely. "No, I don't want to wait, and I don't want to talk about it. Let's go."

Shine grabbed Adam's arm and said, "We could be in danger or in trouble for trespassing, or both." She may have been younger than the other two, but Adam could easily see, no one was going to push her around.

Adam quickly jerked his arm away. "I'm going in," he scowled.

"Come on, Fritzy," Shine urged as she touched Fritzy's arm. "We can get the next bus back home."

Fritzy shook her head and threw both hands up, surrendering her argument. She snapped around to stomp off and then turned back. "Adam Schumacher, when we get back to Sunshine's house, I'm going to call Mom—and she'll probably call Mrs. Gunderman—and she'll no doubt tell your mother."

As Adam turned around, his lip cocked up on the left side and his left eyebrow rose mockingly. "You're going to tattle on me?" Adam's voice rose along with his eyebrow.

"No…Mom will tattle," she stated, her chin turned up defensively. "We're in danger here, and I want some advice," she insisted as she stomped her foot.

Adam's shoulders squared off as he looked at Fritzy defiantly, then they slumped again. "Okay, okay." As he watched the people pile out of the limo, with a little dog tucked under an arm, and enter the Playhouse, he held his breath. "Fritzy, please," he spun around in a final desperate plea. "Just look at them. I have to do this."

"I know you do," she said, her voice still full of anger and determination but aware that he had made up his mind.

She looked again at those entering the playhouse, along with the fluff with the wiggly tail, and gasped. "Spotty?" She covered her mouth and added, "Okay, but, if we get killed, I'm never going to speak to you again."

"Well," Adam drew out slowly, "I wouldn't think so."

"Don't get snippy with me, Adam Schumacher," she spit out. "In the fifth grade, I was the one who kept you from putting the garter snake in Mr. Hamilton's desk drawer." She turned to Sunshine. "Hamilton would have had him expelled. That old man hated snakes."

Shine wrinkled up her nose. "Can't say I like snakes either."

"I know, I know, Fritzy," Adam agreed reluctantly. He looked into her face with pleading eyes. "Please, Fritzy. I have to go in. Whatever Weedy's up to, it's gotta be more than Mrs. Henry's death. With the fence and guards and all, maybe he's a spy."

"Spying for whom?" Fritzy asked. "The United States or Russia?

Adam rolled his eyes. "I see American soldiers, Fritz... not Cossacks."

"Cossacks? Really Schumacher?" Shine mocked. "We just went through World War II, not the Russian Revolution."

"I know, I know," Adam waved her off. "I'm going in there, with or without you two."

"Oh, all right—we'll go," Fritzy agreed and turned to Shine. "This could get us into trouble or worse. You can wait here."

"Wait?" Shine put her hands on her hips and stuck her neck out. "If Spotty is really in there, I want to grab her up and hold her tight. She might be too scared to let you pick her up. I'm coming, too."

Fritzy smiled at Shine and then turned off her grin when she glared up at Adam. "Schumacher, you're stretching our friendship really thin."

"Understood," Adam said cautiously. With his eyes fixed on the playhouse, he led the way around the large enclosure staying close to the trees in the neighbor's yard far up the block. The neighboring house was another estate with wide lawns, full shrubs and bushes and overhanging trees that had begun to leaf out and bloom. There was no sign that anyone in the house even knew others were around. All was silent and undisturbed.

"Let's just hope," Fritzy whispered. Her voice wavered, sounding anxious. "Let's hope no one inside has the time to look out the window at the lawn."

"They hire people to watch the grass grow," Shine smirked. "If they could, they would hire someone to breathe for them."

Way out behind the two estates, the back lot was thick with tall grasses, sculpted bushes and trees that butted up to dense woods. Adam and the girls would have to cross a wide expanse of grass in the neighboring yard to a stand of trees behind the house, before they could cross over to the Runnymede woods. He gestured from their position, to the woods behind both properties, like the military leader of a small army contingent sneaking closer and closer to occupied buildings. He thought of Spenser Tracy leading his men in the movie, *Thirty Seconds over Tokyo*, and wondered again about Pops.

As they crouched inside the tree line, Adam pointed to double French doors with multiple square glass panes at the back of the Playhouse. He knew it wouldn't be a stealth approach. There was too much open space and too many windows. It would take more than fast running and a will to succeed to span that area without notice from whoever was inside the building. He closed his eyes for a second and spoke to his friend.

Shaddi, I know you are here. You have always been with me even when I didn't know it. If anyone is inside the large room, turn their backs to the windows. Silence the little dog, Spotty, and please, make this rescue possible.

Crouching as they ran, they sprinted past bushes shaped in the form of candle sticks and baskets of flowers. Adam payed no attention to the greenery he passed but kept his eyes on the house. If he could have flown in a super invisible airplane, he would have. He would have preferred that it belonged to Superman...just a guy thing. Even though Adam, Fritzy and Shine were right out in the open, there was no sound from the building.

As they neared the Playhouse, Sunshine threw her hand to her mouth to stifle her surprise and excitement. There, looking out the windowed doors, her silly little dog looked up at her, its ears pointed straight up. Spotty's wiggle was so profound she turned herself in circles. Shine placed her four fingers and thumb together quickly, making a fist, an obvious silence command. She looked back at Adam and Fritzy who nodded in giddy agreement.

Shine held her hand to her mouth again and kept her eyes glued to the dog, making sure the cocker would not bark. Adam spoke to Shaddi once more just as Shine touched the handle of the French doors. He and Shine exhaled with relief. All three of them nearly jumped in the air when they found the door was unlocked. Shine silently gasped when she saw that her roomer, Oliver Weedy, was one of the group in the building. Through the crack in the door, Adam, Fritzy and

Sunshine could hear those inside speaking in raised tones with anger in their voices. Their faces, drawn up and obviously angry, turned red with mounting tension as they argued about something.

Thankfully, the house was so grand the door dared not make a single squeak. Adam thought of the rusty hinges on the door to the enclosed back porch of their farm house and cringed. The door of the Runnymede house opened smoothly on silent hinges. Shine opened the door just wide enough to let Spotty wiggle through, scooped up the dog in her left hand and re-latched the door with her right. She didn't look at those inside, just wrapped her arms around the little dog and snuggled her close.

Once Spotty was outside, the three plus dog backed away from the house and kept their eyes on the people they could see through the windows. The inside group seemed to be huddled together in a great discussion. Shine, Adam and Fritzy never looked up, or looked away, or looked toward the door. They darted for the camouflage of the trees. Panting and coughing, they reached the coolness of the leafing vegetation in time to catch their breaths before landing in a pile on top of one another.

It was only then that Adam could pause long enough to take stock of the situation, to actually see what they had just experienced. Out front, the military unit guarding the property clustered together at the front of the estate. Their main task seemed to be checking all trucks and vehicles that tried to come through the gate. Once Adam and the girls were again at the back of the estate in the woods, the three of them looked back at the Playhouse.

"I guess they never thought anyone would try to break in from the rear," Adam said.

Shine gave Spotty another hug. "What is going on here? It sure doesn't look like a ladies' bridge party is happening in the ritziest suburb of Dayton. It's serious enough to kidnap a little dog that never won a blue ribbon or had her picture plastered on the front of a Gaines dogfood can. This whole thing is fishy. Oakwood is not the secret-spy type of town."

Fritzy's eyes rolled. "I thought it looked harmless from the bus-line. Now, I don't know."

Sunshine kept her hand clamped over the dog's nose and mouth like a muzzle as all three stood in the woods of the adjoining property to the right of the playhouse. Still, no one inside the building made a sound. Yes, the teens were in the trees, but not yet out of the woods. They circled around again, out of the woods, through the neighbor's yard, and back out onto the sidewalk farther up the street. Immediately, they turned and ran up the sidewalk toward Far Hills Avenue and arrived just in time to catch the southbound bus.

As they stepped up the three steps onto the bus, the driver put his hand over the top of the fare box. "Sorry, no dogs allowed on the bus."

"Oh, of course not," Adam agreed with a deep bow of contrition. "Dogs do not belong on busses." He slapped his hands together as if he had no more to say, and then added, "But, this little one is a seeing-eye dog. My friend here is blind, or at least blind enough she must have the assistance of her little dog."

"Then why isn't the dog on a leash?" The bus driver's tone was humorless and laced with disbelief.

"Yes, sir. Of course she would have a leash." Adam rubbed the top of the dog's head and felt a wound near her neck. "See, look here. Someone kidnapped her. When they tore the collar from her neck, they left a deep wound. My friend is lucky the dog wasn't killed." Spotty tilted her head and looked up at him with gentle cocker spaniel eyes.

"Blind, huh? You don't look blind," the driver slowly removed his hand from the fare box.

"Oh, thank you so much, mister," Shine gushed. "I want to look as normal as possible, and my little dog helps me to get around just like everyone else. I'll keep her quiet if you let us get back home." She held the dog even closer and kissed the top of her head.

The bus driver said no more. He watched the trio out of the corner of his eye with a wary smile. "Sit down you three. And, keep that dog quiet. I guess all four of you are going. So, sit."

"Come, Sunshine. I'll help you." Adam offered his help, picked up her hand as if she couldn't see it, and placed it in the crook of his arm. "Back this way," he said. "There's the vertical pole and there, the bars at the back of each seat, and then straight back."

"We might have to start paying rent on these seats," Fritzy said with a sullen smile.

Adam settled back onto the side bench seat. "We did. It's called car fare."

"Right," Fritzy said as she folded her arms across her chest and slumped down on the bus bench.

Sunshine watched Fritzy for a minute. "What's wrong?"

"Nothing," Fritzy pouted.

Adam looked at his friend with a puzzled expression. "Wrong? We rescued Spotty and got away safe. I'd say everything is right."

"You would, Adam Schumacher," Fritzy blurted. "You always push things to the danger point."

Adam's eyes widened. "Danger?"

Fritzy's hands flew out in animated expression. "You don't even know the danger we were in, mister. The Runnymede Playhouse was guarded and fortified." She slumped farther onto the bench. "That place was not a 'playhouse.' Those people were either mafia or government."

"Mafia?" Adam gasped.

"Well, you tell me why there were guards everywhere," Fritzy whispered loudly and looked around for those who might be listening.

Sunshine cuddled Spotty closer in her arms. "I'm glad we got her back, but Fritzy is right. With both Wright Field and Patterson Field located here in Dayton, we had all kinds of things going on here during the war. There are gated and guarded installations all over town."

The three of them said nothing for a few minutes but watched the scenery as the bus snaked its way through the suburbs of Dayton, turning off Wayne Avenue and onto Wilmington Pike. Adam tried to redirect the conversation. "What's that big building up there on the hill?" He pointed to a complex of old red brick buildings.

"That's the Dayton State Hospital," Shine answered as she stroked Spotty's soft smooth head.

"State Hospital?" Adam kept the diversion going. "What is that?"

Fritzy looked around for those who might be listening. "I wrote a paper on it for class. It was first built in 1875 and was called Western Ohio Hospital for the Insane."

"Oh," Adam said and thought out loud. "I wonder if Pops could have been transferred to a hospital like that. Someone said he had lost his memory and didn't know his own name."

"I doubt it," Shine said holding Spotty a little tighter as the little dog wiggled in her arms. "He has amnesia, not a mental problem."

"But, you do, Adam," Fitzy blustered.

Adam's mouth flew open, "Me? I have a mental problem? Why Frederica?" he enunciated sharply.

"You heard Shine. There are government secrets behind guarded gates all over Dayton."

Shine straightened up a little. "Well, I don't know about now, in 1946. During the war we were all affected by blackouts and rationing and all."

"The whole country was rationed," Adam reminded her.

"Yes," Shine agreed. "And, blackouts. We'd be ready to go someplace in the evening and the sirens would go off announcing a blackout. We had to turn off all the lights in the house and even stop our car and turn off the headlights until the all-clear siren sounded. If someone spotted an airplane, before they could identify it, they had to assume it was an enemy plane. Turning off the lights made the city and possible bomb targets hide from the attacker."

"Adam, that's what I'm saying" Fritzy insisted. "We don't know what was going on back at Runnymede but it was important and dangerous enough to need guarding. You insisted that we walk right in there."

"How long are you going to be mad about it?" Adam asked sheepishly.

Fritzy placed her hands on her knees and, rocking back and forth, tears gathered in her eyes. "I haven't decided yet, Adam. I'm scared."

Adam reached out to take her hand, but she pulled away and buried her hands in the folds of her arms. "Let me know," Adam sighed. Then he thought about all that had happened that day. He closed his eyes in thought and prayer. *Thanks Shaddi for protecting us at the Playhouse. Now, please let me get information that will lead to the where-abouts of Pops.*

Chapter 20
Oliver Weedy's Surprise

"What the…?" Buddy shouted as he looked in his rear view mirror and saw three figures walking toward them from the rear. "Duck!" he shouted as he slipped under the steering wheel and grabbed Freddy's shirt sleeve. "Quick! Get down!"

"Why?" Freddy barked back and looked over his shoulder toward the corner. "Oh crackers!" he said as he threw himself on the floor of the car. "How—?"

"Shut up, Freddy," Buddy whispered coarsely. "They're passing. The windows are down." Cramped into a taco shaped blob of a person, Buddy tried to fold himself into the smallest space possible.

Adam, Fritzy and Sunshine chattered lively as they walked past Buddy's car, totally unaware of the passengers in the old jalopy with the Indiana plates. Spotty was still in Shine's arms but even she paid no attention to the boys. The three were still so excited about their adventure at the Runnymede Playhouse the rest of the world simply dissolved into a surrounding blur. But, this story had not yet reached its final scene.

"How did they get to take that dog on the bus?" Freddy asked as he looked up and watched them head toward the

Sullivan home. "That guy gets to do whatever he wants, whenever he wants to."

Buddy stared at him in wide-eyed disbelief. "That's your only question?" he sassed. "And, it's about the dog?"

"So the dog riding a bus is a mystery to me," Freddy admitted. "So what? We sat here all this time and they weren't even around, and all that upsets you is a question about a dog?" Freddy whispered loudly.

"I sat here…you slept," Buddy snapped back.

"We don't have buses in Middletown, you know," Freddy grumbled. "I never thought of them taking a bus and leaving without the truck. Did you?"

"Okay…" Buddy drew out. "They're back now. Forget it." He stretched out his arms and legs and tried to unkink himself but decided it would take more time.

•••

"Well, that was a short movie," Grace said, putting down her mending as the three, plus the dog, came back into the house. She parked the needle in Dan's shirt front where she was replacing a button.

"We didn't go, Mom," Sunshine beamed. "We rescued Spotty."

"What? What are you talking about?" Grace's brow furrowed quizzically. But, when Shine pulled the dog from behind her back and reached toward her mother with the little cocker, Grace's mouth bounced open with a gasp. Her arms flew out automatically as she took the dog onto her lap. "Where did you find her? Where was she? Why is she bleeding on the back of her neck?"

Shine bubbled with joy. "While we were going through Oakwood, Adam saw Spotty in the back of that big black car we told you we'd seen Weedy in downtown." She bent over and scratched behind the pup's ear.

"I couldn't believe I saw Seedy Weedy riding in that limo again." Adam shook his head in disbelief and eased himself onto the end of the couch.

"How did you get her home?" Grace continued to ask. "Dogs don't ride buses."

Fritzy plopped down on the footstool at Grace's feet. "We elevated her title to a seeing-eye dog. She played her part very well."

Shine giggled, "I pretended to be blind, Mom. That way we could take her on the bus." She laughed. "I did a pretty good job. I convinced the driver. Maybe I'll try out for some of the school plays this spring."

"You kids …" Grace marveled as she carefully looked at Spotty's wound. "It looks like the bleeding has stopped." She parted the hair on the top of the dog's head. "Shine, please bring the mercurochrome from the cabinet in the kitchen. It's good for people; it'll be good for Spotty, too."

While Sunshine went out to the kitchen, Adam couldn't clear his head—not from thinking of Weedy, but worry about his dad. "Did anyone call for me, Mrs. Sullivan?" He asked hopefully.

"I'm sorry, Adam. I know how anxious you are to get word about your dad. But, no one called, and I was in the house the rest of the day after you three left."

Adam asked another question. "Did the police come around?"

"They drove by and were in and out of Mrs. Henry's house for quite a while this afternoon. Then a little later they came back here with some more questions, but left right away when their police radio went off." Grace took her handkerchief from her pocket and blotted the gash in another wound she found on the dog's neck. "This cut looks like the place where someone probably tore off her collar." She kissed the top of Spotty's head. "The question that Office Gilbert asked that surprised me the most was, if I knew that Mr. Weedy was related to Mrs. Henry. I told him I never heard of such a thing."

"Weedy and Mrs. Henry?" Adam jumped to his feet, scratching his head. "Did you ever see him down at her place?" He paced back and forth and then sat back down on the edge of the sofa. "It can't be a coincidence that the Weedys came to live here with a relative just across the field. But, still, if he had no contact with her.... That Weedy guy is sounding more and more suspicious; but, I don't know what he's suspicious of."

Suddenly, the front screen door banged closed as Oliver Weedy burst through. "Sorry, Mrs. Sullivan," he said sheepishly without looking at anyone in the room. "My wife and I are going to have to move out in a hurry...today." He started for the stairs then turned and looked around the room. There on Grace's lap sat the little dog. "How...?"

"Mr. Weedy, you didn't expect to see Spotty here?" Fritzy asked. Her voice was edgy and bold and her face taut.

Adam jumped up again and took a step in Weedy's direction. "You might also want to know, your cherished relative, Mrs. Henry, was killed sometime last night or early this morning." Adam sounded like a homicide detective, accusing Weedy of something.

"What?" Weedy sank down onto a chair.

Adam's expression shifted from defiant to surprise. "You mean you didn't know?"

"No, I didn't," Weedy whispered. "Killed? She is—or was—my aunt. She only treated people with kindness." He shook his head as if he were trying to clear his thinking. "Are you sure she was killed?"

Grace chose her words carefully. "The police said someone ransacked her bedroom." Then she asked carefully, "What would they have been looking for, Oliver? What would have been in her room?"

"It wasn't there anymore," Weedy whispered.

"What wasn't there anymore?" Adam asked as he sat down and leaned toward Weedy.

"Never mind," Oliver fumbled with his suit jacket. "Forget I said anything." Weedy stood up. "I gotta go."

He turned and ran upstairs two steps at a time. Adam, Grace and the girls could hear him slam the door to his sitting room.

"What is going on?" Grace questioned as Spotty jumped down from her lap.

Just as quickly as Weedy ran upstairs, he flew back down again. He had his briefcase in one hand and a small valise in the other. There was a brown manila envelope under his arm. He placed the small suitcase on the step and the briefcase on the top of the post near the telephone, opened it and placed the envelope inside. "I'll call you, Mrs. Sullivan, and give you our forwarding address. If you will please send the rest of our belongings on to us, I would appreciate it." He pulled his billfold from his back pocket and took out two twenty dollar bills. "This should be enough to take care of shipping the items." Then he looked inside his billfold and seemed to tally up something. "Oh, here is the money for the next three months' rent to cover any losses that you might have from our quick departure." He pulled out more bills and offered them to Grace.

"I think you had better wait until the police have a chance to question you," Adam cautioned. "Mrs. Henry being a relative of yours and all." He got up and stepped in front of the door, blocking the exit.

"Now son," Weedy warned, "you don't want to get in the middle of something that is way bigger than all of us. Step aside."

"I can't do that," Adam said defiantly, his arms folded across his chest. "A lady was killed—your aunt. I'd think you'd care more than…just leaving."

"How do you know she was killed? She might have just died from old age." Weedy started to pick up the cases again. "She was old."

"She was old, yes. But, that's not what killed her," Adam insisted, his eyes fixed firmly on Weedy. "She was shot in the back of the head. I saw where the bullet entered her skull." He did not budge but planted his feet more firmly on the hardwood floor. "And, what did you mean when you said *it wasn't there anymore*? What wasn't there anymore?"

"It's none of your business. Now get out of my way." Weedy kept his hands to his sides; but his fingers moved constantly. Though his eyes shifted from one person to another, he did not move farther away from his briefcase.

"I can't let you get past," Adam insisted. *Shaddi, give me the power of Superman, and the speed of an arrow.*

You know I'm with you, my son, Shaddi whispered in Adam's heart.

Weedy reached into his inner jacket pocket, pulled out a pistol and waved it at all of them. The gun shook in his trembling hand. It was obvious from his expression he was losing control. His face contorted in tight, drawn muscles and narrow lips that froze his face in a mix of fear and panic. His eyes twitched and Adam wondered how long it would be before the gun went off during a muscle spasm. He'd seen many movie with scenes just like this one and they usually didn't end well.

"I couldn't find the mercurochrome at first," Sunshine blurted out as she came back into the living room. She froze in mid-step when she saw Weedy's gun.

"Over there, Adam," Weedy motioned with the revolver. "Move over there…you too, Sunshine. I don't want to hurt anyone. You know that. Rather than killing the little dog, I took her with me; didn't I? She wouldn't stop sniffing around the front room."

"What did you have in that room?" Adam asked. "The only thing the dog would be interested in would be a roll of salami." Adam didn't move. He held his position at the door.

"You don't want to know," Weedy said as he choked on his words. "Your life would be in danger just like mine is, if I gave you any more information." He waved the gun around, motioning for Adam to sit down.

Still, Adam didn't move.

Weedy cocked the gun's hammer back.

Shaddi! Adam called out in his mind. Instantly, Adam leaped forward from a standing position and flew directly at Weedy's legs. With his left hand, he chopped at Weedy's right hand and knocked the gun out of the man's grip. Weedy fell to the floor. "Fritzy, grab the gun, quick!" Adam yelled.

Black shadows oozed out of Weedy's pockets, rose above him and sat on his back. They cackled as they jabbed at his ribs and head. No one saw them but Adam. Weedy would have only felt the immense energy drain from their attack.

With the presence of the dark shadows, Adam knew just how evil the man was.

"Oh, dear me," Mrs. Sullivan screamed. "What is Aunt Arletta gonna say when she hears about this?"

"Mother!" Sunshine screamed. "Call the police, hurry!"

Adam clumped his clodhopper on the back of Weedy's neck and held him down. He grabbed the black telephone from where it sat on the post and swung it over toward Mrs. Sullivan. The receiver became detached from the base but the long cord Mr. Sullivan had attached when they moved to the suburbs reached all the way to where Mrs. Sullivan sat frozen in her chair.

Grace placed her finger on the hook bar until she got a dial tone. With shaking hands she dialed the police department. Her eyes darted back and forth between Adam, who had Weedy pinned to the floor, and Fritzy, who was only a few years older than Sunshine, but was holding a loaded gun on Oliver Weedy.

"Hello?" Grace paused and tried to clear her voice as it cracked. "This is Grace Sullivan again over on Keystone Avenue. We have an emergency here. Come quickly. Adam, our young friend, has subdued the man who may be involved in Mrs. Henry's death. Fritzy, a girl of only fifteen, is holding a gun on the man." Grace's eyes were wild and frightened. She paused again. "Okay...hurry."

Grace tried to replace the receiver as she trembled. "He said that I should hold the gun on the man until they arrive. They'll get here in a matter of minutes. There's a squad car on Wilmington Pike right now."

"Mother," Sunshine whispered insistently. "You have never held a gun in your life."

"Has Fritzy?" Grace asked in a frenzied gasp.

"What?" Weedy tried to raise himself up but Adam's boot kept him pinned.

"Oh, yes," Adam said with a smile of triumph on his face. "Frederica Bremen goes hunting with her father every year, and has since she was nine years old. Don't kid yourself, Weedy; she knows exactly what she's doing. I'm not sure if she's had a chance to go hunting as often as she would like to this year. But, I wouldn't get her riled. She might think you're a deer."

A siren wailed again as the squad car came down Keystone Avenue and pulled into the Sullivans' driveway. The screen door banged as Officers Gilbert and Young ran in with their guns drawn. Grace startled and jumped.

"You can take your foot off the guy now, son," Gilbert said as he grabbed the man off the floor and searched him for additional weapons. To Officer Young he said, "He's clean."

"I did not kill my aunt, Mrs. Henry," Weedy insisted.

"Then why did you pull a gun on us?" Fritzy asked with a snap as the officer relieved her of the revolver. "And, what do you think happened to Mrs. Henry?"

"Will my wife and I get a deal from the prosecutor if I tell you what I know?" Weedy asked Gilbert.

"As long as you repeat it word for word when there's a stenographer to take down your statement," Gilbert agreed. "I'll tell the prosecutor you cooperated with us."

"Okay, okay," Weedy turned as the officer jerked him around by the arm. "I work for a company as a chemical engineer. Some men contacted me and wanted me to infiltrate the Manhattan Project here in Dayton. And, I'm telling you that I had nothing to do with my aunt's death. I had managed to get some papers smuggled out and hid them in a dug-out at the end of the road. Then, I hid them down at my aunt's house.

She didn't even know they were there. The other day, I moved them back to my apartment and locked them in the desk. That dog over there," he scowled at Spotty, "kept sniffing around. I couldn't risk her finding anything. If you're looking for who killed my aunt, try the guys who dragged me into all of this."

"What kind of papers did you steal?" Officer Young asked as he shook his head. "Things like this don't happen in Beavertown."

"I can't tell you very much about it because it's top secret. But, I can tell you that they wanted the Polonium triggers that are used in the atomic bombs."

"Atom bombs?" Gilbert growled. "Mister, I just got back from the war. I don't want to relive it right here in my own neighborhood."

"The Manhattan Project?" Adam asked. "Does it have anything to do with the Runnymede Playhouse?"

"I don't know what you know about the Playhouse," Weedy tensed, "but I warn you, you'd better forget it."

"Are you threatening this young man?" Young asked as he reached for his service revolver.

"No, sir, I am not," Weedy denied immediately. "But, just knowing as much as he does, could be dangerous. The Sullivans have been nice to my wife and me. I don't want any harm to come to them," he explained.

"No harm?" Fritzy snapped back. "You pulled a gun on us."

"What does your wife have to do with all of this?" Gilbert asked.

"She works for a patent attorney in Dayton. She was supposed to try to get some paperwork out of that office and into my contact's hands."

Officer Young rubbed his chin. "What papers would be downtown?"

Weedy winced as he struggled with his story. "Evelyn hid our contract with the "spies" in the safe at her office. No one would search there since that office is not connected in any way with Runnymede."

Adam blinked and stared at Weedy, trying to put everything together. "The patent to the Polonium triggers? And, the triggers have something to do with the atomic bomb?" He blinked his eyes in confusion and spun around.

Officer Gilbert shook his head and gritted his teeth. "You mean to tell me that the patents to bomb components are right here in Dayton, Ohio? Why here? Why not in Washington DC?"

Weedy bit his lip and squeezed his eyes shut. "Monsanto is here. They are building a completely underground complex in Miamisburg. It will combine all of the Manhattan Project Units from around Dayton into one place. They nearly have it completed."

Grace's eyes grew large. "Miamisburg? Ohio? All Units—down the road a few miles?"

"Never mind all that," Weedy denied. "Forget I said anything," he insisted.

"The patent?" Sunshine repeated. "In our house?"

Weedy exhaled loudly, "No, it's not the patent for the Polonium triggers. That is elsewhere. It's..." he swallowed hard, "it's the blueprints."

"You were at Runnymede to do...what?" Adam shouted in disbelief.

"The Polonium triggers were developed and assembled at the Runnymede Playhouse."

"Right there in the lovely suburb of Oakwood? At Runnymede?" Grace gasped in complete disbelief.

Weedy twisted as the officer held him even tighter. "They needed the blueprints at first when they were developing them. Then, they stored the blueprints in a big safe until they needed to make more triggers." He cleared his throat and added, "I took them out and Evelyn had them copied. I'd gone to Runnymede to put the originals back."

Fritzy's eyes bulged with fresh understanding. "And, the triggers were hauled out in big trucks!"

"Right." Weedy shook his head in desperation. "Now, let's drop it all."

"No," Adam insisted. "What are your contacts' names?" Then his eyes widened. "Who are they?"

Weedy raked his hand through his disheveled hair, hung his head and squeezed his eyes shut. "I can't tell you those guys' names," he gasped. "They'll kill me."

Adam straightened up and pulled back his hand in a fist. "Well, when they come here in the middle of the night to kill us," his voice rose to a shrill, "I'm sure the police would like to know who to look for."

"They wouldn't come here," Weedy denied, shaking his head in disbelief. "They wouldn't know I had brought the blueprints back here to the house; that Evelyn took them downtown for copying; and that I had put them back in the desk again until I could return them to the Playhouse safe."

Fritzy put her hands on her hips. "They came close enough. Just a few yards down the street. And, they killed your aunt." Her eyes grew narrow and her face red with anger. "When they didn't find the blueprints at her house, they'll eventually come here. You know they will. Doesn't life mean anything to you—or the life of your aunt? Didn't you care anything about Mrs. Henry?"

"Of course I did. I loved her," Weedy snapped back.

Gilbert pulled handcuffs from his belt with a forceful jerk. "Give us the names, Weedy." He forced the cuffs over Weedy's wrists, causing his briefcase to fall to the floor. Paper bound packets of money flew all over. Weedy's face turned white.

Gilbert put out his hand and barred Adam and his friends. "Nobody touch any of it. We don't want any fingerprints on the money, except Weedy's. We'll call in an evidence-gathering expert."

"The names, Weedy," Fritzy demanded. "Who are they?"

Weedy shook his head back and forth. "They will catch us all before anyone can catch them."

"The names," Gilbert insisted.

Weedy sighed deeply in resignation. "Joseph Kruger and Carl Turner." Then he stopped and dropped his head again in defeat. "My wife," he breathed out in whispered desperation.

Officer Young's brow furrow more deeply. "Where is Mrs. Weedy now?"

"I called her at the office and told her that there had been a break in at the Playhouse." He nodded in Spotty's direction. "I knew the little dog was gone from the Runnymede location and had to assume she got out when someone broke in. We had no idea that these kids had somehow found the dog and rescued her without knowing anything about the operation there. My wife and I talked about it and decided there would be investigations, and we had better get out of town. She's waiting for me to pick her up."

"We'll save you the trouble," Gilbert laughed. "We have friends in the Dayton Police Department, and even the FBI, who can pick her up for you. Now, isn't it your lucky day?" Gilbert turned to Adam with a stern gaze. "I want you three to stay in the house here with the Sullivans. You are not to leave their sight. Got it?"

"I hear you," Adam sighed. His eyes snapped to attention. "Officer, what have you found out about Mrs. Henry's murder so far? How long will this take? I have to go find my father."

"Nothing until now. But, like I said, stay close. I'll have to question those two—Kruger and Turner—before I'll know more." He paused and looked at the disappointment of Adam's face. "All right. If you get a lead on your father, let me know when you leave, where you're going and a contact phone number."

"Okay," Adam agreed. "Lucky day? I wish today had been my lucky day and Pops was going home with me," Adam said, stuffing his hands into his pockets. But, that's not all he said. Inside his head, another conversation was going on. *Sorry, Shaddi. I won't wish for things. I'll wait for you to make it right with Pops.*

Chapter 21
Information About Pops

Morning came early for Adam. How could he sleep after all the events of the previous day? Adam, Fritzy and Shine had entered Oliver Weedy's apartment against the rules of the rooming house. The Sullivan family dog, Spotty, had gone missing. They found Mrs. Henry dead in her little house down the street. Dark shadows oozed out of every crack in Mrs. Henry's house. While going into town, they followed a lead about the dog, only to find a top secret atomic bomb research and assembly facility. Then, a nervous traitor held them at gun point. Sleep? Not last night. Hungry? That was something else altogether different.

Adam jumped up off the porch glider, went into the house, darted up to the bathroom to wash, hurried down and into the dining room and emptied a plate full of pancakes.

"More flapjacks coming up," Grace called from the kitchen. When she got to the table, she slapped two more warm cakes on each plate. "Is there enough syrup and butter?"

"Yes, Ma'am," Adam said as he reached for the butter plate. "Did Mr. Sullivan have pancakes before he left for work?"

"Dan likes a couple of eggs, toast and coffee for his breakfast," she said and smiled.

"These are wonderful, Mrs. Sullivan." Fritzy smacked her lips and wiped her chin on her napkin where maple syrup had developed a drip track.

"How many can you eat, Adam?" Grace asked.

"I'll slow down here in a minute," he grinned, knowing full well he could have eaten a mountain of the golden hotcakes. He wanted Mrs. Sullivan to sit down and enjoy some breakfast, too.

"I'm full," the girls sounded out in unison.

Grace went back to the kitchen and put the remaining batter on the griddle. She returned with two more pancakes for Adam and two for herself. "These are good," she said as she savored the first bite.

When the doorbell rang, Sunshine jumped up from the table. "I'll get it."

At the door, she stopped. "Adam," she called over her shoulder as she let a man dressed in a military uniform into the house.

Adam patted his mouth on a napkin and excused himself from the table. When he was still six feet away, he stuck out his hand in friendship when saw the man. "Sergeant, I'm glad to see you. Sorry, that's really Captain Smith. How did you find me?"

"I'm fine with *Sergeant,* Adam. It feels like a nickname for a favorite uncle."

Adam chuckled and added, "If you're sure. But, you are a captain."

"The war's over, son. I don't need a rank now. And, as to how I found you, you gave me the phone number for the Sullivan house. It was a Walnut exchange, that's Beavertown. So, I called the police out here and asked if they had heard of the Sullivan family." Sergeant Smith smiled and winked.

Adam smiled. "Please Sergeant, sit down."

The Sergeant continued. "The officer questioned me, asking if I've heard of the Sullivan family. They said, their daughter and two guests, Adam Schumacher and Frederica Breman, found a dead body and caught part of an espionage ring yesterday." Smith shook his head in amazement. "You people were famous by this morning."

Grace brought in a cup of coffee and handed it to him. "How about a cookie to go with the coffee, Sergeant?"

"Thank you for the coffee," Smith said as he took the cup in both hands. "I'll pass on the cookies, but I do thank you."

"This is my mother, Sergeant, Grace Sullivan," Sunshine said. "Do you need any sugar or cream for your coffee?"

"No, I don't," Smith said and smiled. "But, thank you very much...again." He sipped from the cup of hot coffee and then asked, "Adam...an espionage ring? What has been happening?"

"Part of the Manhattan Project was located in some buildings and facilities around Dayton," Adam began.

"The Manhattan Project?" Smith's voice rose in alarm. "The bomb? Here?"

"The bomb," Fritzy stated emphatically.

"A roomer here in the Sullivan home was asked to steal the blueprints to the Polonium triggers they used in the atomic bombs," Adam explained.

"Polonium triggers?" The Sergeant stared in disbelief. "What do you kids know about the Atom bomb?"

"Absolutely nothing," Fritzy joined in with a bewildered look on her face.

"What I just told you," Adam admitted with his palms turned up empty, "is the end-and-all any of us know about bombs. But, here we are, right in the middle of it."

Smith looked at Mrs. Sullivan. "So, has this roomer been captured?"

"Well, yes. Oliver Weedy is in police custody, and they picked up his wife as well," Grace said with a sigh. "It's the other ones, the murderer, or murders, who haven't been caught yet."

"Murderers?" Smith gasped and nearly spilled his coffee in his lap. "Who died?"

"Weedy's aunt," Sunshine said and added. "She lived next door, on the other side of the vacant lot."

"The kids found her," Grace explained. "And, I feel so bad about that."

"You don't have to feel guilty, Mom," Shine blurted out. "You didn't kill her."

"Sunshine!" Grace shrieked. "What a thing to say."

"What?" she exclaimed loudly. "I said you *didn't* kill her."

"So…" Smith jumped in between the mother and daughter, "the real killers could be anywhere."

"Yes, I suppose," Adam stated in deep thought. "No, I don't just suppose. Of course they could but we can't do anything about that. That's not why I'm here." He had to redirect the conversation to the whole reason he was in Ohio. "Did you find out anything about Pops?" He asked as he slowly sat down on the very edge of the chair and leaned toward his friend.

"Yes…and no," The Sergeant answered as he sipped his coffee. "This is very good, Mrs. Sullivan."

"Yes…and no?" Adam's expression fell as his heart sank to his stomach.

There had better be more yes than no. He fought inside with the demons of old who had robbed him of his security and respect for his own father.

Adam's mind raced. *Pops is not a traitor. That fear has haunted me, embarrassed me, and tried to tell me who I am for months now. I don't know where he is, but I have to find him and prove it to everyone.*

"Let's do the *yes* part first, Adam." Smith placed his cup and saucer on the end table. "I went through all the records at the VA and the man who may be your father, the one I told you about, was moved from our Dayton location to a half-way house up near Columbus. His body is well. Actually, his mind is well, too. He doesn't have dreams, depression or anxiety. He simply cannot remember his life before the Battle of the Bulge. So, the *no* is, no—he is no longer in the Dayton area, but yes, he is still in Ohio."

"How did you get all of that information?" Grace asked.

"As you know, I work at the VA Hospital. Actually, I'm a doctor but work as a social worker right now. The U.S. Medical Department did employ some Negro doctors, and nurses as well, who worked in the all-black hospitals and back-wards of white hospitals where Negro patients are treated. Most physicians of color were also ambulance workers. Yes, Mrs. Sullivan, as a VA physician, I have access to all of the files."

"Then, you must be Sergeant Doctor Smith," Grace said as Smith smiled wide and shook her hand.

"Something like that, thanks Ma'am," Smith joined in the fun. "Actually, my rank is higher but everyone calls me Sergeant."

Adam was still turning over in his mind all of the things Smith had just said. "Wow, Easter break will be over soon. How will I be able to find Pops and bring him home?" He hung his head in disappointment.

"Columbus is about eighty miles north and east of here. This is only Wednesday. You can still do this, Adam," Smith encouraged him. "I'll make contacts for you. Give me a little time."

"I'm going, too," Fritzy chimed in. "I won't be left out when you're so close."

"Are you sure it won't be too dangerous," Adam spit out sullenly in Fritzy's direction.

"Alright, Schumacher," Fritzy snapped back. "That's enough."

"Me, too," Sunshine added and then looked at her mother. "Aren't I?"

"There wouldn't be room for Pops in the truck if you both went," Adam sighed. He wanted the company. Fritzy had been with him through it all and now she wasn't talking to him very much. She usually talked all the time and he needed that hum in the truck.

"If you wait until three-thirty when Dan gets home, I think he'll let you use the sedan, Adam. Dan will use your truck for work while you're gone. He's not a truck kind of guy, but this is important." Grace sat on the piano bench and sipped her coffee. "Rev. Bob Powel and his wife Barbara used to be the youth workers at our church. They live in Columbus now. I'll call them and see if you kids can stay with them or at their church while you're in Columbus."

"Oh, Mom." Shine jumped up and gave her mother a hug. "You are the best."

"Well, your dad will have to agree first," she warned with a smile. "But, he's the one who insisted that you and your sister be raised to be independent and able to get around on your own." Her eyes fixed on her coffee as if there were tea leaves in the bottom to help her form a plan. "After you get your father, Adam—and you will get him—you'll drive back here with the car and Sunshine, and pick up your truck before you head west. I'm pretty sure Dan will give his blessing. And, you will of course call me at least once a day. Fritzy, what about you? This is a decision your parents will have to make, not me."

"They know I'm safe and in good hands," she said and stole a quick glance at Adam.

"Safe?" Grace raised her eyebrows and her volume. "Just yesterday, you had to hold a loaded gun on an enemy of the state!"

"You held a gun on someone?" Smith questioned. His brow furrowed into two deep ruts between his eyes.

"Yes, well, I guess that's true," Fritzy admitted. "But, you'll have to admit, I did it very well." She kept her eyes off Adam and added. "Danger has been around several corners."

"Please, make all the phone calls necessary," Adam said. "When Mr. Sullivan gets home, I'm heading for Columbus. I would love to have your company, girls. But, I will go, with or without you two." He glared at Fritzy, making sure that she heard the seriousness in his voice. "And, I will bring my father home."

"I know you will," Smith said as he got up to leave. "But, whatever you do—be safe. There is still a dangerous person out there."

•••

Later that afternoon, the teen trio sat on the front porch and stared out across the driveway to the side yard where butterflies fluttered from the budding cherry trees on the far side of the yard, to clusters of blooming roses, and waited for Sunshine's father to come home from work. It was an unusually warm day. The peony bushes in the yard on the other side of the driveway were full of pink blooms and the tulips beside them had opened their blossoms to the blue sky. But, all that Adam could think about was Pops.

If Sunshine's voice hadn't been so quiet, she would have startled the other two out of their reverie. "He leaves for the Frigidaire really early, before I even get up," she mused. "He should be home soon."

They all said no more for a few minutes. Waiting was hard. Somehow, having Mr. Sullivan home would make everyone feel less anxious. It would settle one issue in the multitude of events that had happened.

"It smells like fried chicken," Adam whispered in their shared afternoon daze. He may have been lost in thought but his stomach was always alert to the demands of the next meal.

"It is," Grace said from inside the screen door. "You three will have supper before you leave."

"Mama," Shine perked up as a grin spread across her face. "Meat again?"

Grace pushed the screen door open, came out onto the porch and slipped down onto one of the green metal tulip shaped porch chairs. "During the war, we only had meat on Sundays," she explained. "Since the war's been over, we have tried not to use more than our share. Today seems like a celebration so—meat it is."

"Yes, Ma'am," Adam agreed. "We'll leave after we've helped you with the dishes."

"I'll accept that help," she said as she threw her tea towel onto one shoulder. "As long as you three are on the road by five-thirty or six, there will still be plenty of daylight by the time you reach Columbus." She tapped Sunshine on the knee. "You make sure you call me as soon as you get there."

"I will," Shine agreed then reassured her mother by patting her hand. "There's Daddy," she called out as the 1938 brown, four-door Dodge pulled into the driveway.

Dan drove slowly into the garage, got out and walked toward the porch. At the porch steps, he stopped. "Well, is this a welcoming party?" he asked.

"Sort of," Shine said as she began the long explanation that led to the question about the family sedan. "So, what do you think, Daddy?" she asked.

Dan Sullivan was a hard-working man who began his years in the factory at the age of fourteen. Few people could take advantage of him, which made his generosity a surprise at times. "Well, okay," he agreed. He turned to Adam, "How long have you had a driver's license, young man?"

"A license?" Adam asked. "About a month or six weeks," he explained hesitantly as he watched Dan eye brows climb up on his forehead. "But, now wait, sir. I've been driving the tractor on the farm and then the grain truck since I was nine."

Dan's smile spread across his face. "Well now, that sounds good to me," he laughed. "Sunshine, you be sure and call your mother soon as you get there."

"I already promised," Shine agreed.

"Adam, you call your mother too before ya leave," Dan added. "Let her know what's happenin'."

"Yes, sir, but that would be a long distance call," Adam reminded him.

Dan smiled. "I know that, son. But, your mom still deserves a phone call, don't she? It's my phone, my home, and my dime. I can work an extra few minutes next Saturday to pay for the call if that makes ya feel better."

The corners of Adam's mouth turned down. "Not better if you have to work more...but I'll call Moms before we leave, if that makes *you* feel better."

"More important, it will make your ma feel a lot better," Dan said as he sniffed the air. "It smells like fried chicken," he said as he closed his eyes, apparently seeing the dinner table in his mind. "I hope you're plannin' to stay for dinner." He opened the screen door, started to walk in the house and stopped. "Grace might even be able to whip up some dessert if we're lucky."

"A chocolate cake with fudge icing is waiting on the counter," Grace announced as she followed Dan into the house.

"That convinced me," Fritzy said as she jumped up and followed them in. "Mrs. Sullivan," she called after Grace, "I'll help set the table for a larger piece of cake than Adam's."

"What?" Adam shouted after her. "I'll even mash the potatoes if there are any to be smashed. But, I claim that huge piece of cake."

"Wait for me," Shine demanded with a giggle. "This is my house, my mom and therefore my cake." She bounded into the house.

•••

"Adam, you might as well have that last chicken leg," Dan offered, wiping his fingers on his napkin.

"Thank you, sir, but I can't take more than my share," Adam said as he blotted his mouth. "You're the bread-winner. You've worked hard."

"Boys need more food than most other creatures," Dan laughed. "When I was younger than you, I started workin' in a factory. My foreman would bring me a milkshake about 10 AM and another one about 2 PM. He said if I was gonna do a man's job, I'd havta fatten up a little," he smiled a smile of memories. "I was a skinny kid."

"You might as well take that last leg, Adam," Grace said. "You can't out argue Dan Sullivan."

"Daddy can argue that it's raining outside while the sun is shining—and win," Shine added with a tone of mixed experiences—both triumph and defeat.

"While you polish off that chicken, I'll get the cake," Grace offered. "Shine, bring your ruler. You can help me cut the cake in mathematically equal pieces."

"Oh, Mother," she whined dramatically with drooping shoulders—then grinned at Adam and Fritzy.

Adam picked up the last chicken leg from the platter and took a bite. "This is so good, Mr. Sullivan. When Moms was in the tuberculosis sanitarium I had to find food wherever I could."

"Sorry to hear that, son," Dan said. "But, you've gotta admit, all that livin' on your own did make you grow up fast."

"Yeah," Adam agreed and thought about his months in the belfry of the church. "It sure was a lonely way to finish growing up."

"You're probably right," Dan agreed. "I guess I really wouldn't know. I went to work at a young age, but I had five brothers and sisters to share bread with when work was done."

"Here we go," Grace announced as she and Sunshine brought in small plates of the chocolate-on-chocolate dreamy dessert and passed them around.

"Now wait," Shine began. "Don't start eating yet," she said as she sat down with her piece of cake in front of her. Slowly, she picked up her dessert fork in her right hand and tapped the firm fudge icing. "Notice...the icing is firm to the touch and the consistency of yummy chocolate fudge." She carefully lifted the tip of the icing where the piece made a triangular point. "If you lift slowly," she instructed with a firmly set mouth, "you can actually remove a piece of fudge from the top and eat it like candy." She delicately raised a firm chunk, held it out to study the rich piece, and bit off a generous chunk as she closed her eyes. "Oh wow...amazing."

Adam drooled a little as he watched the perfect execution of dark fudge extraction. Adam studied the technique, picked up his fork and dove into the cake, icing and all. He closed his eyes in anticipation and popped the forkful in his mouth. When he opened his eyes, he apologized. "Sorry Shine, I couldn't wait."

Dan threw back his head and laughed. "Now there is a man who appreciates good eatin'."

As Fritzy cleaned the last few crumbs from her plate, she said, "I have all my stuff ready, Adam." She looked at her watch, "It's getting late."

"Good honk," Shine gasped as she glanced at her Mickey Mouse watch. "It's five-thirty, and we promised to help with the dishes."

"Well," Dan drew out, "you kids need to get on the road. Shine, I'll help your mother with the dishes."

Shine's fork clattered as she dropped it on her plate. Grace's eyes grew large, and she nearly choked on her last bite of cake.

"Daddy," Shine gulped. "I can't remember you ever helping in the kitchen."

Grace jumped in quickly. "We're not criticizing. In fact, we're thrilled...aren't we Sunshine?"

"We sure are," Shine said as she quickly picked up her plate, glass and silverware and took them into the kitchen. "Come on guys, bring your stuff in. At least we can do that."

"Thank you one and all," Grace sang out.

"Here's the keys, Adam," Dan offered as he picked up his own table service and brushed any crumbs from the tablecloth onto his dirty plate. "With six kids at our house when I was growin' up, my job was to sweep the floor after each meal." He put his arm around Grace's shoulder as he started through the swinging kitchen door. "This could be fun."

The sound of dishes slipping into the soapy water of the large wall mounted sink filled the back of the house. Grace pulled the draining rack and drain board from under the little black linoleum covered white cabinet beside the sink and placed them on top of it.

As Adam took his dishes out to the sink, he watched the wonderful play and chaos around the kitchen. He wondered how his life would have been if he had brothers and sisters. Something like his experience there in the Sullivan's kitchen he guessed. It was a good day and he knew it. Now, it was time to leave.

Chapter 22
Pastor Bob

Adam, Fritzy and Sunshine piled into the old Dodge sedan and slowly backed out of the driveway. Grace and Dan sat on the porch glider enjoying a little bon voyage send off. The spring early-evening air was crisp and clean, like freshly cut grass from the Skroggen lawn across the street. Sunshine said Mr. Skroggen was either working on his car with *vroom vroom* sounds, or mowing the yard with a finely sharpened push-mower, his car radio blaring out country music. After work today, it had been the grass that occupied his time and attention, and perfumed the air.

"Bye," Grace waved to the kids. Dan reached over and put his arm around her as they glided.

Adam and the girls said their goodbyes out the car windows. They started off with Fritzy beside him in the front and Sunshine in the back seat. As they neared the turn at Harvest Avenue, a plain black four-door sedan pulled out of the little over-grown driveway down at Mrs. Henry's house. The driver, with dark, round rimmed glasses and his passenger, in a grey fedora hat, slowly rolled up the street, just far enough back to go unnoticed. No one inside the Dodge paid them any attention.

Unnoticed by everyone, Buddy and Freddy brought up the rear. "Oh, that car had to pull between us," Buddy complained. "Wow, Schumacher goes from truck, to bus, to sedan. Keep your eye on the car he's driving now. Make sure it doesn't get away from us." The boys in the junky jalopy were completely unaware that they were the third car in the little parade that pulled out onto the pike.

●●●

"Okay Adam, how are we going to get there?" Fritzy asked when they were on Wilmington Pike. "Did you write down the direction Shine's dad gave you?"

"Right," he said as he pulled a piece of paper from his shirt pocket and handed it to her.

Shine jumped in. "I remember Daddy said to take Far Hills Avenue into Dayton so you'll have to turn left onto Dorothy Lane. That's up here, a little past the Beavertown church," Sunshine offered as she watched Devon Avenue pass by and then the church.

Fritzy read over the directions carefully. "I'll navigate, if you want me to," she offered and studied Adam's face.

Adam looked right and left before turning at the light onto Dorothy Lane. They rode in silence for the next few blocks, and then Adam turned his body right again—this time, so he could get a glimpse of Fritzy. *What's going on with her?* He asked himself but he didn't ask her. Fritzy should know him well enough to tell him if she was mad or something. When he stole the look at her, she appeared more relaxed than she did the day before. Maybe the storm had passed.

"I'll review the directions quickly and then remind you step by step," she suggested. "Far Hills Avenue, which is Route

48 into Dayton and it's Main Street downtown; then turn east onto E. Monument Ave."

Shine offered from the back seat, "You'll recognize Monument because there's a huge war memorial statue right in the middle of the intersection." She reminded them, "You'll remember having seen it when we were in town before. You can't miss it."

"Oh yeah," Fritzy agreed before going back to her list of turns.

"Then what?" Adam asked.

"Okay," Fritzy began again as she moved her finger down the list. "East to North Keowee Street and follow that road north to Ohio Route 4. Then you'll connect with Route 40, going east, through Springfield."

"Then, Columbus," Adam and Sunshine said together.

"Sergeant Smith gave me another set of directions," Adam said as he patted his shirt pocket. "Route 40 will take us to the north side of Columbus. The half-way house, or group-home, is up there."

Fritzy was quiet for a minute and then asked, "Is the group-home a facility of the VA?"

"No," Adam answered slowly. "Smith said a lady whose husband was killed in the war, decided to open her large farm home to men who were ready to leave the hospital but weren't ready to go to their homes. Her son graduated from high school and he helps with activities."

"That's swell!" Sunshine stated in amazement.

Fritz turned and threw her arm over the back of the seat. "That's a little like your folks, Shine. They opened their home to returning military who couldn't find housing."

"Right," Shine agreed.

"Didn't you say, your mom's cousin's husband—Catherine's Dave—was in the Army?" Adam asked.

Shine thought for a moment. "I didn't think about it like that. A half-way house describes it—half way between the war and their home."

•••

Adam pulled into a service station within the city limits of Columbus. "I'm going in to call Rev. Bob Powel. It's only fair to let them know we're nearby."

"We'll be right here," Shine said as she yawned. "I'm going to close my eyes."

Adam had parked off the concrete apron that stretched around the gas pumps so as not to block cars as they tried to pull up to get gas. The girls waited in the car beside the strip of grass next to the street. Long shadows danced along the lawn across from the station and warned everyone that the sun would set soon.

In a few minutes, when the service station door closed, Fritzy announced, "Adam's coming." She had opened one eye and forced the other to blink into focus as well.

"Great!" Adam's voice nearly cracked as he opened the door and slid onto the seat. He fumbled with the car key and used both hands to insert it into the ignition. "Pastor Bob said they live just a couple of blocks from here. They're in the parsonage to the left of the church."

"What?" Shine drew out through a groggy haze.

"It's good," Fritzy bubbled. "We're close to Pastor Bob and Barbara Powel's place. I'll be so glad to get out and walk around a little. My legs are stiff."

Adam started to say that she could have gotten out of the car while he used the telephone, but he caught his words before they splattered all over everything. As he watched Fritzy, she continued a rapid-fire explanation of how glad she was to be almost there.

"I'll race you around their house, Schumacher, as soon as we say our proper glad-to-meet-ya's. I bet I'll win," she laughed.

"I don't think we can run in their home," Adam teased but he knew what she meant. He was so happy to have his old friend back from her dark and angry mood, he couldn't resist.

"I'll join you two in that race," Shine perked up. "So, don't collect your trophy before we get to the finish line."

Adam pulled back onto the road and followed the directions Pastor Bob had just given him on the telephone. The whole area was beautiful farm land, at least Adam knew of nothing more perfect than a plowed field or one in which the winter wheat was nearing harvest. Several miles and a few turns later they had arrived at Powel's parsonage.

"Look," Shine pointed to a man standing by the edge of the road out in front of a house. "It's Pastor Bob."

It was easy to see the smiling minister ahead of them. His glow led them forward. Adam recognized his good spirit from a distance. He followed the pastor's lead as Bob directed him into the driveway at the side of the house. It was a square, white brick house with brown shutters and brown door. It looked warm and homey. Columbine grew beside the front steps, with budding red bell-shaped flowers. Their backward-pointed nectar tubes waited for hummingbirds to get their fill. Adam smiled as he thought again of Rudy.

Leaning in the car window, Bob smiled broadly. "Just leave the car here and come on in the house. Barbara had me make homemade ice cream and it's been packed and ready for eating for about a half hour. Let's dig in."

"Glad to help you out, sir," Adam grinned and offered his hand. He was always ready for ice cream, homemade or store bought. He thought he could taste it already.

"Our race can wait until later," Shine suggested. Turning to her former youth pastor, she added, "Hi Pastor Bob. These two had challenged each other to a race to work out the car-kinks—Adam Schumacher and Fritzy Breman."

Bob threw his head back in a hearty laugh. With a sweep of his hand, he said, "There's the church parking lot. It will make a nice flat surface for running and the street lights will be on in…" he checked his watch and added,"…in about twenty-five minutes." He slapped Adam on the back and gave Shine a hug. "Welcome," he said to Adam. "Good to see you again, Sunshine. Tell me all about your trip. From what Grace told me on the telephone, you three have had several pretty challenging days."

"A challenge puts it mildly," Shine agreed. "We're living our lives inside a mystery movie—with us as the stars—or the victim. The jury is still out on that."

"A race track for our sprint? Perfect," Fritzy jumped in. "Schumacher, prepare to be beaten. Jiminy Christmas, fearless leader, you have been running on empty for days, chasing government spies all over Dayton." Then she added as she tapped her finger tip on his shoulder as she passed, "You are going down."

Adam's grin was hard to hide and he wondered why he even thought of hiding it. He and Fritzy had been friends for as long as he could remember. All of a sudden, he was feeling silly around her, like a twelve-year-old forced by his mother to go to his first boy-girl birthday party.

"Come on inside," Barbara Powel called from the front door. "Let the kids get washed before we dish up our ice cream." She smiled as the three approached the front steps. "Bob always finds someone to talk to. My young friends, it is your turn today."

"All right," Bob laughed as he ushered the three into the living room.

The room looked comfortable to Adam. The furniture was lovingly-used and well balanced in the room. Soft leather chairs, worn to a chocolate and butterscotch patina, flanked the fireplace. A light blue couch faced the hearth and a huge round chunky wood coffee table occupied the negative space in the triangular center.

"If you'll excuse me—" Barbara said as she went out into the kitchen. "I'll get the ice cream."

Shine jumped up and followed her. "May I help you?" The two chattered as they walked through a door into the kitchen.

"Adam?" Barbara shouted from around the kitchen door. "Can I talk you into a big serving?"

"Yes, Ma'am," he called back with a large grin.

"I hope you don't mind, Adam," Pastor Bob began, "I called the half-way house your Sergeant described and asked them about their routine."

Adam looked up in surprise. "Oh? What did they say?"

"Yes, Adam," the pastor assured him, "I am interested in your mission to find your father." He leaned forward and rested his hands on his knees. "Your expression tells me you feel alone in this."

"Maybe...a little," Adam admitted. How could he admit he had felt alone for more months than he wanted to admit?

Fritzy sat beside Adam on the sofa. She reached over and put her hand on his shoulder. "Adam, you know I believe in you. I've been beside you all the way…except of course when I was under the tarp in the back of the truck."

Fritzy's hand felt warm and it gave Adam comfort…and something else. He wanted to put his hand on hers…but he didn't. He didn't know why he was acting so funny.

"You are not alone Adam" the pastor assured him. "You have friends and family who are rooting for you. And, remember, God is with you all the time."

Adam thought about Shaddi, his comfort and his friend. Even the little hummingbird stayed in the church tower with him and didn't fly south with the rest of his flock.

"I know God is with me and he has been with me all along," Adam acknowledged. Then he whispered, "I can't think it through. I don't understand. But, I know he's there."

"Ding, ding," Shine sang out. "The Good Humor men or ladies in this case, are here." She and Barbara brought in a tray full of ice cream bowls. Shine handed a bowl to the pastor and Barbara gave ice cream to Adam and Fritzy. With their own bowls in hand, Shine sat on the hearth and Barbara took her place in the second leather chair.

Adam scooped up a large spoonful of ice cream, then remembered the brain freeze he had the last time he ate homemade ice cream too fast. He took a deep breath and relaxed. "You were saying, Pastor…about the half-way house?"

"Right," Bob said as he dug in for another spoonful. He swallow hard and then pinched the skin between his eyes. "I talked to Johnny Trumbull. He said his mother has breakfast for the men early and they finish by 8 AM. She agreed to let you stop by any time after that, until noon when she serves lunch. The same with the afternoon—one to five PM, then supper."

"What about the girls, Fritzy and Shine? Can they come with me?" Adam asked as he ate another bite.

"I asked Trumbull about that," Bob said as he enjoyed a little more of the ice cold treat. "Johnny said it would be fine for the girls to come along." He paused and put the spoon in the bowl. "Adam, I would be happy to go along with you guys...if you want me to."

"That would be great, Pastor. Since you made the contact, they know you already," Adam added as he wiped sweet cream from his chin.

"They sound like easy folks to get to know," Pastor Bob assured him.

"Thanks," Adam said with a sigh. "I needed to hear that." He studied his ice cream bowl for a moment. "I would be happy for you to come along. I have no trouble meeting new people. It's just that it's getting so close to finding Pops, I'm getting all shook up inside."

"I understand," Pastor Bob assured him. "Remember, God will be with you."

"I know," Adam admitted. "It's just that I've waited so long, now that the time is almost here, I feel like I'm rattling inside."

Shaken or not, Adam knew, tomorrow would be a big day. He was positive he would find his father. He simply had to.

Chapter 23
The Race

Later that evening, Adam toed up at the start line and crouched in position. He looked neither right nor left. He knew Fritzy was on his left and Shine his right but he didn't care. He would be the first off the line and the first over at the finish. He'd show Fritzy Breman who had the power to win.

Why have I started having to best Fritzy in everything? He wondered to himself. *We're friends—not competitors.*

"Go!" Pastor Bob shouted from the other end of the parking lot.

The three tore out toward the bicycle with the yellow handkerchief the pastor had tied to the back wheel so the runners could easily identify the winner's mark. As they neared the finish line, Fritzy surged ahead by one stride as Adam began to dive for the yellow with Sunshine close on their heels.

Adam was not going to let anyone pass him. He pressed forward and crossed the finish line. Fritzy began to laugh in the fun of it all and thrust herself forward. Losing her balance, she plowed into Adam from the side just as he burst across to his goal. Fritzy stumbled into Adam and Shine fell into both of them. The trio piled into a mass in the grass at the side of the parking lot as Pastor Bob jumped out of the way.

"Wow," Sunshine exclaimed as she jumped up. "Did we tie? It sure seemed like it."

"No," Adam yelled. "I won."

Fritzy laughed and tried to tickle him as they rolled on the grass. "Say it Schumacher. I won."

Adam grabbed his side, pretending he couldn't catch his breath. "Okay…okay, I'll say it," he laughed. "I won."

"No!" she shouted again.

Adam jumped to his feet and offered his hand to Fritzy. With a snap and a pull she flew up and into his arms. His stomach felt funny and he wasn't sure if he liked the feeling or not. He caught a glimpse of Pastor Bob who, with a knowing smile, winking at him. Adam let go of Fritzy, hopped back and brushed off his jeans. "We'd better go in," he said as he smacked at his cheek. "The mosquitoes are starting to bite."

"Good idea," Pastor Bob said as he patted Adam on the back. "Barbara has made up the guest room for the girls and a roll-away in her sewing room for you Adam."

"Thanks, sir," Adam offered as he continued to brush off grass and imaginary insects from his clothing.

As the girls walked back to the house ahead of them, Pastor put his arm around Adam's shoulder. "Looks like you're getting bitten by several things, young man," he said as he laughed.

"I know. It's all a little confusing," Adam admitted.

"I understand," the pastor said. "You need to know, it won't get any better."

•••

As the lights went on in the upstairs bedrooms of the parsonage, a plain black car pulled into the dark corner of the paved parking lot and the driver turned off the lights.

"We'll sleep here in the car tonight," the man in the glasses said. "We want to be able to follow them when they leave."

The other man reached in his jacket pocket. "When we stopped at the service station back there on the corner, I bought some candy bars." He handed a Babe Ruth to the driver. "Here, enjoy your supper."

Unnoticed by the two men, Buddy had parked his wreck-on-wheels in a driveway a few houses up the street. The people there had posted, "Florida for Easter or Bust" across the front window. The house was dark and all was silent.

"No one's home," Freddy said. "Wish my family and I were going to Florida."

"Your family never goes anywhere together," Buddy snapped back sullenly.

"Neither does yours, Buddy," Freddy sassed. "At least, we have families," he whispered. A new softness was beginning to round out his sharp and jagged edges.

Chapter 24
The Next Day

The morning sun rose behind a grey fog of spring rain that had fallen during the night. Adam had already gotten up and was down stairs on the porch. Taking in the fresh morning air, regardless of its thickness, was a habit of farm-life he saw no need to break.

Shaddi, I'm going to need you today if I'm going to see Pops. You were with me through it all, now be with me today, please.

"Morning," Pastor Bob called out as he stepped up on the porch. "I've had my walk and talk with God and I'm ready to take on the day."

"Me too," Adam grinned and thought again of Shaddi.

"It sounds like the rest of them are up," the pastor laughed. "I hear girl chatter."

The two walked into the house and met the others around the kitchen table. Barbara had placed a cereal bowl at each place. "If you'd rather have cold cereal, the boxes are there," she said as she pointed to boxes of Wheaties and Cheerios in the middle of the table. "And...I have hot oatmeal over there in the pot on the stove. Help yourselves to whichever you want. There's also brown sugar and a few nuts for the oatmeal."

"It looks wonderful," Adam said as he inhaled the sweet steam from the pot. "Moms made oatmeal every winter morning." He took a bowl from the table and filled it over the stove. A spoonful of brown sugar sprinkled cross the top and another measure of nuts and it was ready for the thick sweet cream. Fritzy was right behind him at the oatmeal pot and Sunshine chose cold cereal.

Pastor Bob offered a blessing after they gathered around the table. Everyone dug into their breakfast in silence. Adam's first spoonful was like a visit home, a holiday for his mouth. He had missed so much, even though Moms was out of the hospital now. The texture of the oats brought back the taste of family.

When they finished eating, they were ready to head out. "We can take my car," the pastor offered. "We have a woodie wagon. It's old but seats six and is still comfortable."

"But, sir...,"Adam began.

Bob put his hand on Adam's shoulder and whispered, "Son, I am praying that you will be able to bring your father home. You will need the larger transportation. Let's be prepared."

Adam's voice choked up as he thought of the possibility of even finding his father. Now, Pastor Bob was speaking a prayer, asking God to actually bring Pops home.

They all stormed out of the house, a small contingent of military personnel on a serious mission, and piled into Bob's car. Adam sat in the front seat with the pastor while Fritzy and Shine occupied the center row. They all chatted eagerly about the task at hand. No one saw the empty dark car near the tree line. As the Woodie pulled out of the parking lot, two men rose up from their hidden position slumped down in the front seat of their car. Once the Woodie had cleared the lot and turned the corner, they started their car, pulled out and followed a half-block behind them. The two-car parade rolled on.

Chapter 25
Steve

Twenty-two forty-one Gumm Street sat on forty acres of farm land north of the capitol city of Ohio, Columbus. The large house, balanced on a little knoll by tall oaks and walnut trees, sat surrounded by hydrangea and lilac bushes. A man on a green tractor was just turning into another crop row on the wood line of the side-forty. Everything looked clean, pastoral and serene.

"Here it is," Adam whispered with a voice in a battle between hope and fear.

"Look Adam," Fritzy gasped in amazement. "The bank barn looks like the one on your family's farm."

Pastor Bob pulled into the long lane and coasted toward the house as Adam studied the barn with the two ground level entrances. It was red of course, as most mid-west barns were. The huge doors at the top of the earthen, grass-covered hill were open, exposing very old log timber-barn framing. A small flock of sparrows flew from the open doors and took to the top of an oak tree near the windmill. A green hand pump with the name F.E. Myers sat in the space under the windmill. Adam wondered if the pump spout dripped like the one back home on the farm and felt home-sick.

On the road, a plain black car pulled to the side of the berm and came to a stop. The driver rolled down the window and the two men watched Adam and the others as they hesitated, then got out of the Woodie. Black shadows oozed from under the hood of the dark car and danced on the surface.

Like something from a Warner Brothers spy movie, Buddy pulled his car into the grassy entrance of the adjoining woods. More shadows crawled out and sat on the roof of their car. From their vantage point, Freddy and Buddy watched and waited; the black car was unaware of the jalopy and the rattle-trap was oblivious to the grown-up sedan.

At the house, Pastor Bob stepped back and waved his hand, indicating that Adam should take the lead. "We're right behind you, son."

"Right," Adam acknowledged while his heart pounded and his mouth went so dry he couldn't spit. He walked up onto the farm house's wrap-around porch and stopped. Who would open the door? Would Pops stand beyond the threshold? What would he say about not coming home? Adam made a loose fist and knocked on the door.

"Good morning," a friendly lady with white fuzzy hair said when she opened the door.

"Good morning, Ma'am," Adam said as he tried to see past the woman into the house.

"I'm Bob Powel, Mrs. Trumbull," the pastor said as he extended his hand. "I talked to you on the telephone about this young man's father, Will Schumacher."

"Yes, please come in," she offered as she opened the door wide. An aura of bright light rose above her and filled the house.

"Mrs. Trumbull," Adam began as soon as they were all in the house. "This is Frederica Breman, my friend from Middletown, Indiana. And," he pointed with a thumb over his shoulder, "this one is Sunshine Sullivan. Fritzy and I are staying with her parents for a few days."

Mrs. Trumbull took Fritzy by the hand and led her over to the sofa. "You all have a seat and I'll get us some lemonade."

"You don't have to bother, Ma'am," Adam insisted as he sat down on the footstool.

"It's no bother," she said as she headed out of the room. "It's already made."

"May I help you?" Shine asked.

"Well...yes, you may, dear," Mrs. Trumbull said, paused and waited for Shine to join her.

"I don't see anyone around," Adam said, his voice dragging like knuckles on the ground.

Mrs. Trumbull came back in with a large tray in her hands. Shine was close behind with some glasses. "The residents are all out working on the farm." Mrs. Trumbull said and then paused. "There are six men. We have six bedrooms here, two residents per room. Johnny has a room to himself, then there's my room and the sixth is the office." She studied Adam and added, "They don't have to work, but work is therapy. It gives the men a purpose when they've forgotten theirs."

"We live on a farm, Ma'am," Adam explained. "My Pops has worked the land all of his life. That is his purpose."

"That's wonderful, Adam." She poured lemonade into five glasses. Shine carried them over and passed them to Mrs. Trumbull's visitors.

"Thank you, Ma'am," Adam said as he took the glass and sat it on the coffee table in front of the couch. He reached in his shirt pocket and pulled out a small snapshot. "I have a picture of my Pops." He handed the picture to Mrs. Trumbull. "This is Pops. Do any of the men living here look anything like him?"

"Well now, let me see," Mrs. Trumbull said as she took the picture and studied it for a minute. "I couldn't say for sure—he is much thinner now."

"Who?" Adam asked as his stomach began to churn.

"The hospital gave him the name, Steve Farmer because all he talked about when he was first released from the POW camp was farming, crop rotation and what the price of a bushel of corn was."

"Where is he?" Adam asked.

"He's tilling the north acreage." She said and looked at the clock on the mantle. "Steve will be in shortly to wash up for lunch."

"Mom?" a male voice called from the kitchen.

"In here Johnny," Mrs. Trumbull called in the general direction of the back of the house. "Come on in."

A tall twenty-something man with unruly red hair came into the living room and kissed his mother on the cheek. His jeans, folded into a cuff, covered the top of his work boots. Adam thought he looked like a regular guy.

"Johnny, this is Rev. Powel who called about one of our residents here at the farm," Mrs. Trumbull said. "Adam and his friends are hoping he's Adam's father."

"Yes," the younger Trumbull said, "I remember. We've said nothing to any of the men of course."

"Of course," Adam agreed, but deep down he wished the Trumbulls had told the men. He hoped that one of them had said, "Yes, I remember now." Adam said nothing, however, and sipped on his lemonade.

"Any of you know someone in a black sedan?" Johnny asked as he gestured toward the road beyond the lane. "In the country, we tend to notice strangers. It's an old frontier habit of protecting your property and watching out for your neighbors."

"No," they all chimed in together. "Not around here anyway," Fritzy said. "But then, Adam and I aren't from around here."

"Yes, sir," Adam agreed with a grin. "Seems to be the way with country folks—those away from the protection of the city." At least, it was certainly the way his family and the farms around them looked out after each other.

"Well, somebody is parked up there with the motor running," Johnny added as he looked out the front window. "Reminds me of a who-done-it flick down at the Bijou." He chuckled as he looked again at the three teens. "You kids haven't done anything that would call out the goon-squad, have you?" He laughed again.

Adam looked at the girls and sighed. "We haven't done anything, but we know someone who sure did plenty." He watched Johnny's expression change and quickly added, "But, we didn't come here to talk about that."

"The kids have been through a lot in the last two days," Pastor Bob said. "They found a dead body, accidently walked in on a secret government installation and held a traitor at gun point."

"Oh, my goodness," Mrs. Trumbull gasped.

"Fritzy held the gun," Adam explained matter-of-factly. "I don't like guns, unless there's a fox in the chicken coup or something like that."

"You? A young thing like you?" Mrs. Trumbull's eyes grew large and round as she sized Fritzy up.

"Yes, Ma'am," Fritzy said as a huge smile crossed her face. "I go hunting with my father once in a while. Been doing that since I was ten."

"You certainly have experienced more than most adults, except those in the war." Mrs. Trumbull stopped and thought a minute. "When Steve comes in, it may not be good to just approach him like a long lost son, or dad in this case. Why don't you four join us for lunch and gradually introduce yourselves to Steve."

"I hear the back door, Mom." Johnny said as he listened. "They're coming in now."

"Mrs. Trumbull?" a male voice called from the kitchen. "You'd better come in here. I think the biscuits are about done."

Startled, Adam jumped to his feet. "That's Pops," he whispered. "I know his voice." His heart pounded in his chest so loudly he was sure that the one called Steve would be able to hear it from the other room.

"Slow down, Adam," Johnny cautioned with a tampering gesture of his hand. "You can't rush up on him. I don't know what his reaction will be."

"I understand," Adam said but could not, under any circumstances, sit back down. He was long past ready to wrap his arms around his pops.

"Okay," Mrs. Trumbull responded to the voice in the kitchen. "I'm coming. If you think they're done, you can take them out of the oven."

"I did," the man called Steve announced as he came into the living room.

Adam's pounding heart leaped in his chest and his hands began to tremble. The man who stood before him was thin but fit; his chestnut brown hair now turning grey. Beneath hooded blue eyes that sank into dark pools, there was a twinkle that was distinctively Will Schumacher's. Adam's throat closed and he could not speak as tears welled in his eyes.

"Steve," Mrs. Trumbull began, "I'd like you to meet Adam Schumacher and his friends.

Adam extended his hand and smiled with tears rolling down his face. He took Steve's hand in his and felt the warmth he had almost forgotten. It was the familiar grasp of Pops' hand in his, many years ago, as they walked back from the barn on a cold night after checking on a new calf.

"Schumacher?" Steve asked. "That name sounds familiar." He looked at Adam with piercing eyes. "Did I know your family?"

Chapter 26
Lurking on the Outside

Out on the street, the man in the fedora hat reached for the door handle. "Come on. I'm not sitting here any longer. I want to know what's going on in there." Kruger took off his hat, reached back and tossed it on the back seat. "Turner—move."

Carl Turner grabbed Kruger forcefully by the arm. "Joe, are you crazy? We can't just walk in there without a plan. We don't know how many are in there."

"We'll find out when we get in there," Kruger scowled but didn't move.

"And, what if each one who lives there comes dragging in, one at a time?" Turner asked as he waved his hand in the direction of the front door. "It's supposed to be some sort of group home. You hear that? Group! That indicates far more than one or two. And, some are ex-Marines," he yelled with a muffled stage voice. "They may be a little bit nuts, but I'll bet they haven't forgotten their armed combat training."

"Okay, okay, we'll wait a few more minutes."

"Tell me again, why we have to go in there with guns blazing," Turner demanded. His voice dropped at the end as he turned and stared out the window.

"You already know why, Carl. Those kids live in the house Weedy and his wife live in. They probably know everything. They found that old lady. Her little shack of a house is the place Weedy had hidden the blueprints for the Polonium triggers. The Polonium triggers! Carl—the Manhattan Project—the A-bomb! Down at that little three room house!"

"I know, I know," Carl panted as he tried to plead his case.

Kruger gripped the steering wheel tight until his knuckles turned white. "Carl, you were at the old lady's house, too. You know what we had to do. When she woke up and saw us, we had to kill her."

"We didn't *have* to," Carl insisted.

"YES, we did," Kruger insisted. "We had to get those plans and the Henry lady was going to call the police."

"We could have pulled the phone cord out of the wall," Joe said as he tried to make his point.

"She saw us, Carl. She could identify us to the police," Joe growled through gritted teeth.

"Joe, she was blind!" insisted Carl.

"We don't know how much she could see—how blind she was. Maybe it was just distances. We were up close." Joe pounded his fist on the side window. "The street was quiet that morning, while everyone was in church, so no one saw us. We know those plans weren't in that old house. Then, I saw the kid carrying plans up from the end of the street past her house later that morning, after the church hour."

"Joe, how could you tell that the guy had the plans, our plans, from where we were watching up there on the next corner?" Carl shook his head in disbelief.

"The blue legal paper, smart guy," Kruger growled. "A kid that age doesn't walk around carrying blueprints all bound up in blue legal paper."

Turner sighed deeply. "You're right," he admitted.

Joseph Kruger adjusted the gun holster strapped to his chest, just to the front of his underarm, buttoned his suit jacket and opened the door. Carl Turner did the same and stepped out of the car. Carl squared his shoulders and fell in step behind Kruger as they started down the drive.

•••

"Hey," Freddy pipped up from his half-awake position leaning on the passenger side window and poked Buddy on the shoulder. "Where are those two going?" he pointed to the two men in suits as they walked up the driveway. "What's up with them?"

"This doesn't look good, Freddy boy," Buddy agreed. "They look like Edward G. Robinson and James Cagney approaching the headquarters of Big Boss Malone."

"The guy at the service station said this is a halfway house for veterans from the war who couldn't leave the war behind," Freddy said, although Buddy already knew it. It was like the two were trying to make sense of it. They had come to jab at Adam and watch his disappointment when he wouldn't find his dad. "This was supposed to be payback for the know-it-all. But, I don't know about these two clowns."

"For some reason, these guys don't look like clowns. They look dangerous," Buddy said as he choked on the words.

Freddy watched the men a few more seconds, then added, "What can we do about it?"

"Do?" Buddy snapped back. "Nothing—I guess." He squinted out the windshield into the noonday sun.

"Nothing?" Freddy's face muscles began to twitch. "No, Buddy. That's not true," he insisted. "We always do nothing."

He looked out the window again and blurted out, "I don't want to sit on my hands one more time."

"You want to go down there and get into all of that whoop-la when we don't even know what's going on? Freddy, you're crazy."

"I am not," Freddy said as he started to bite the fingernails on his first two fingers and then stopped. "I am finally standing up to you."

"Wow! You really are, Freddy," Buddy's said as his mouth hung open.

"I want to be more than a lap dog," Freddy Alexander demanded.

"You never sat on my lap," Buddy denied.

Freddy socked Buddy on the arm. "You know what I mean." He paused a minute. "I'm at least going up there and try to see something in the window—with or without you." He opened the door and slipped out, crouched low and took a deep breath."

"If you're determined to go up there," Buddy's voice sounded resigned to the adventure, "I guess I'm going, too."

The boys studied the house, driveway and fields. It looked tranquil, a gentle pastoral scene from a Currier and Ives picture. But, Freddy felt something else in his gut. To tell the truth, relying on their street-smart instinct is how both boys had avoided punishment for all their antics in the past. Freddy knew they would have to listen to their guts again this time.

Chapter 27
The Shadows

Inside the house, Adam and his friends joined the Trumbulls and their residents around the large harvest table in the dining room. Adam ran his fingers over the smooth hand hewn surface of the table and thought of his grandpa. Gramps' workshop had a wall full of hand-held, carpenter planes all hung by size and the profile they edged in the wood. The table trim reminded Adam of another time not long ago. One October Gramps made a harvest table just like the one Adam now sat at, so there would be plenty of room for all the aunts, uncles and cousins when they came for Thanksgiving dinner. Now, in a far different place, he looked over at Pops and wondered if his father would ever remember any of it.

"Let's see," Agatha Trumbull said as she studied the seating arrangement. "Adam, I'd like you to sit there on the corner and Steve, you can sit across from him. It seems you two may know the same people and perhaps you can reminisce about old times."

"That would be great," Steve said as he took the chair on the end opposite Adam. Fritzy sat beside Adam with Sunshine next to her and Pastor Bob beside Steve. Agatha took her place at the head of the table, Johnny at the foot and the other men gathered around her.

"Pastor Bob," Agatha said as she folded her hands in front of her on the table, "would you please bless the food?"

"Thank you Mrs. Trumbull—"

"Agatha," she encouraged him.

"Thank you, Agatha," he bowed slightly and smiled. "Let us pray."

Adam lowered his head but kept his eyes open ever so slightly. He could not take his sights off Pops, even if Pops didn't know he was Pops. Adam had dreamed of this moment for so many years and now that the precious time had come, he couldn't even throw his arms around Pops and welcome him home.

Pastor Bob prayed that the food would bring health and strength to all of those gathered around the table. He prayed that those lost in darkness would find their way out by the light of God.

"Thanks Bob," Agatha said as she reached for the biscuits. "Now, for those who have not eaten good Ohio food, I'll pass the biscuits. You can butter it and eat it like bread, or you can build an open face sandwich with the biscuit as the base." She demonstrated. "Break the biscuit in half," she began. Picking up a bowl of mashed potatoes she continued, "Put potatoes on top and then a generous helping of creamed chicken." She ladled out two scoops of the creamy chicken. "Add salt and pepper to taste."

"Wow," Adam's smile spread across his face. "Moms makes chicken like this."

"Moms?" Steve asked, his face drawn into a distant memory.

Suddenly, an awful stench coming from the front of the house over-powered the delicious aroma from the steam rising off the gravy bowl. Adam began to gag and covered his mouth with his napkin.

"Are you all right, Adam?" Agatha asked.

Fritzy started patting him vigorously on his back. "It's that awful smell coming from outside," she said as she grabbed her stomach.

"You smell it, too?" Adam asked, amazed. He knew it was the dark shadows but they had never been that strong before.

"I sure can smell it," Shine joined in as she pinched her nose with her fingers.

Everyone at the table began to gag and put their hands over their mouth and nose like they too could smell what only Adam had detected in the past. How was it possible? Granny O'Hara had told him about the dark shadows in the glen near her home in the bog of the east. It was their secret. The shadows had followed him home to Indiana. He thought they were dangerous only to him.

When the door banged open, Adam nearly blacked out from the incoming smell, like a smoldering city dump on a sweltering summer night. He gasped and gagged as Joseph Kruger burst into the room, his pistol drawn in deadly aim. Carl Turner was right behind him. He needed two hands to hold the revolver in his trembling hands, but he kept his aim.

"Shaddi," Adam whispered in desperate need.

"El Shaddai," Steve called out and then looked at Adam, stunned.

Kruger and Turner said nothing at first but seemed to circle around the table, stalking their prey. "Where are they?" Kruger finally demanded.

"What?" Adam asked.

"Who are you?" Fritzy asked; the corner of her upper lip turned up.

Sunshine silently wrapped her fingers around her fork like a dagger. "What do you want from us? We have no money. I have a dollar and a quarter left over from our gas money."

"I think they're Joseph Kruger and Carl Turner," Adam concluded as he pulled his butter knife from the place setting and slipped it into his lap under his napkin.

"If you know who we are, kid," Kruger growled, "you know how dangerous we are and what we're looking for."

Each diner around the table looked at the others in bewilderment. No one moved.

"You can stop with the act," Kruger growled with a vicious snarl. "The blueprints—we want the blueprints. Now!"

"What blueprints?" Agatha asked as she studied the faces of the veterans around her table. "These men have been through a lot," she cautioned. "Many suffered from chronic Shell Shock. The images of war rattle around in their heads and bring the same fear those scenes did during battle. Please, put the guns away and let's talk."

"Listen to her Carl, a do-gooder who thinks talk will solve everything," Kruger sneered. "I mean it. Give me the blueprints," he shouted and shot at the floor one inch from Adam's foot. Dark shadows belched out their vile pungent smell as they danced around the room cackling and parading their evilness. They slithered between the chairs, under the table, and swung from the chandelier.

Immediately, in a burst of lightening, two young strangers flew in through the door behind the men and tackled the gunmen like defensive linebackers. At the same moment, Adam shot across the room, his arms spread out, aiming at Turner and the loaded gun. Turner spun around and fired. One of the two strangers screamed in pain, fell and grabbed his leg. The battle-hardened veterans at the table jumped into action and surrounded the two gunmen, a mighty army of six in full assault.

"Freddy!" Adam and Fritzy yelled above the chaos of flying fists.

Adam knew neither Buddy nor Freddy ever played football, so the whole gridiron scenario they had displayed was amazing. Adam lunged again for Turner, a super hero in flight, while Buddy rolled over on top of Kruger, wrestling with him for his gun. The gun twisted and turned in their hands as they fought for ultimate possession. With Adam still in the middle of the tangle, Turner fired, grazing Adam's arm above his elbow.

"Adam!" Steve screamed and flew into the fight. Landing on top of Turner, Steve began pounding him with his fists, over and over, until the gun flew from his hand and landed near the table. Bob Powel grabbed the revolver off the floor and held it on all of them.

"Okay, let's sort this out." Bob waved the gun back and forth, separating all of the arms and flying legs.

"Adam," Steve gasped again as he went to the boy's side.

"You know me, Pops?" Adam cried as he struggled to his feet.

Will Schumacher placed his hands under Adam's arms and helped him up. He checked Adam's wound first. "It isn't deep," he said. Looking into Adam's eyes, he grabbed the boy and embraced him. "Son," he wept on his shoulder.

"Sheriff?" Agatha spoke into the telephone. "This is Agatha Trumbull, out here on Gumm Street. You'd better hurry. We've captured two men with guns after they broke into our house." She paused and listened. "Good." She replaced the receiver and looked at the men, all of whom were holding down Turner and Kruger. "There's a car in the area. They'll be here in a few minutes"

Fritzy dove for Freddy who still lay on the floor, holding on to his leg. "Freddy Alexander, let me see your leg." She pushed up his pants leg as he let out a scream. "I am so sorry," she apologized as she lifted his jeans more carefully. When she got to the bullet wound next to his shinbone, she quickly removed her head band and wrapped it around his leg. "The authorities will be here soon." She tied off the band. "What on earth are you two doing here?"

"Never mind all of that," Freddy blushed. "It's a long story and not a very honorable one at that. I'd just as soon forget about it."

"You're the hero of the day, Freddy," she said. "You saved us all. If you don't want to talk about why you're here, no one's gonna make you. We're just thankful you came." She looked over at the others. "Buddy, are you okay?"

"I sure am. Bruised but—" he said as he hung his head. Looking up he added, "Feeling better than I have in a long, long time."

Adam watched as dark shadows gasped for air and oozed back outside, through the screen door. They slithered off the porch like wounded vipers, hissing their dirge of pain out into the yard where they seeped into the dirt and mud from where they came. Luckily, no one but Adam saw the retreat of evil. Nothing should dampen the triumphant joy of subduing the enemy and of celebrating the return of a war hero.

Will Schumacher looked around the room, seeming to see it all for the first time. "Adam, is your mother here?"

"No Pops," Adam said slowly. "She—has had tuberculosis, Pops—"

Will grabbed at his chest and inhaled deeply. "My Bridget! Is she—?"

"Oh no, Pops," Adam quickly interrupted. "She is out of the sanatorium. She and I have been living in a little guest cottage belonging to friends. She's just still weak and dare not even catch a cold."

"Thank the Lord," Will sighed out, like he had been holding his breath for too many years.

Fritzy looked over at Adam who was still talking with his father. "Mr. Schumacher?" she asked.

Will let go of Adam with one arm and put it around Fritzy. "Frederica Breman," he answered. "You came all the way over here with Adam to bring me home? You are a real friend."

"Most of the time," Adam said as he laughed. "She's been grouchy lately."

"I have not, Adam. It's been him, Mr. Schumacher. He's been taking risks and putting us in danger."

"Anything like today?" Will asked.

"Maybe you don't want to know that part just yet," Fritzy said. "But, trust me, it has been lively and Adam keeps pushing the limits."

"Maybe he wants to show off for his best girl," Will suggested and winked at Adam.

"Best girl?" Fritzy asked as her cheeks grew hot and red.

"Yeah," Adam admitted with a defiant tone, his chin turned up. "Best girl—if that's okay with you, Fritz." He reached over and grabbed Fritzy by the waist and drew her into his arms. "You still want to go to the Spring Fling when we get home?"

"I sure do," she laughed and rolled her eyes. "I sure do."

Chapter 28
Back in Beavertown

"Sunshine," Adam announced as he turned onto Keystone Avenue, "you're home." He and the girls had already dropped Bob Powel and the Woodie off at the parsonage in Columbus. When Adam, Fritzy and Sunshine, plus his dad, Will, arrived back at the Sullivan home in Beavertown, they had a couple extras with them. Buddy and Freddy followed in Buddy's old heap while Adam drove Dan's sedan.

"Come on in," Shine invited the two misfits as she got out of the car. "You're part of us now. Come on in."

"Oh...I don't know," Freddy hesitated as he looked at Buddy who remained behind the wheel. "I don't think we'd better."

"Well, at least come up on the front porch, and I'll bring out some sweet tea," Shine offered.

Adam studied the boys and scratched his head. "I don't know why you two are so shy. You both flew in like Superman and knocked the gunmen off their feet. Freddy, Turner's bullet hit you in the leg. You had to have it removed in the Emergency Room. And, Buddy, you sat on Kruger and held him down."

"Why are you so nice?" Freddy asked. "We treated you like—well, we treated you bad. How can you act like nothing happened?"

Will Schumacher grabbed hold of the driver's door. "Come on." He stepped back so Buddy could get out. "I forgot everything, guys. I couldn't even remember my own name, Adam, my wife Bridget, or any of my life in Middletown. Adam was a better man than me. Where you two are concerned, Adam *chose* to remember no more—just like God forgives us and chooses to forget all we do that separate us from him."

"So...you're like God?" Buddy asked Adam, his eyes bugged and his mouth open in surprise.

"Hardly, Buddy boy," Adam shrugged and popped Buddy on the shoulder. "I didn't really get to know you two guys very much at school or around town, but I didn't dislike you." He paused as he wondered if he should continue. "I just thought you guys were...lazy fools."

"Hey!" Buddy drew back his fist in a defensive move.

"Stop," Freddy wrapped his hand around Buddy's fist and stopped him. "He's right, Buddy"

Buddy jerked back. "So—you're on his side now?"

Will smiled and said, "Isn't it nice that there aren't sides any longer? The war is over."

"There has to be sides," Buddy insisted as he twisted away and slumped down on one of the steps leading up to the porch. "How do you know when you've won?"

"Won what, man?" Adam squinted as he tried to understand Buddy's thinking.

"Someone always has to be on top," Buddy insisted. "One is a leader and the others follow."

"Not in a friendship," Will said as he sat down beside the boy on the step. "In a friendship, both are equal or it isn't a friendship at all"

Buddy said nothing. Adam did notice a change, however. He watched as Buddy's back straightened and his face softened. To Adam' thinking, that was good enough for a beginning.

"Welcome back, everyone," Grace said as she came out onto the porch.

"Mother, we have a few more with us." Sunshine pointed to Will. "This is Adam's father, Will Schumacher."

"Mr. Schumacher," Grace said as she extended her hand. "I am so very happy to meet you." She took a handkerchief from her apron and blotted the tears that welled up in her eyes. When Dan followed her outside, she turned to him. "Dan—I'd like you to meet Adam's father, William—Will Schumacher."

"Will," Dan threw one arm around Will's shoulder, "I'm glad you're finally home."

Will patted Dan on the shoulder and said, "I'm getting there."

"We'll be heading back to Indiana in a little while," Adam explained. "Pops will find his full way home when we get to the farm."

"Mom and Dad," Sunshine turned and bowed formally, "I'd like you to meet Freddy Alexander and Buddy Phillips. They're friends of Adam and Fritzy."

"Well, I wouldn't…" Buddy started to undo his new relationships.

"I would," Fritzy darted in between Buddy's words.

"Me, too," Adam added.

Grace offered her friendship and shook Freddy and Buddy's hands. "Pastor Bob called and said you two were vital to getting our daughter home safe." She reached out and threw motherly arms around Freddy. "I cannot thank you enough." She expanded her embrace and pulled Buddy into the huddle.

Both boys were stiff and awkward with Grace at first. As Adam watched them, they began to melt and return her appreciation with hugs of their own.

Dan checked his watch. "I gassed up the truck for ya, Adam."

"You didn't have to—"

"Of course I didn't have to, Adam. I wanted to," Dan insisted. "It's five P.M. Grace has fixed a nice supper for everyone." He looked at Buddy and Freddy and restated forcefully, "For everyone." He smiled broadly and stuck out his chest. "I have agreed to help Grace do the dishes, so you four, and you two boys, can be on your way by six."

"Dishes again?" Shine gasped. "Daddy, you are really trying to impress Mom," she said with a teasing grin.

"Any way I can," Dan said and laughed as he gave Grace a sideways hug.

"Oh, you," Grace blushed as she wiggled out from under his arm. Then, she began to direct the group in two directions. "The Weedys are gone, so anyone who wants to use the bathroom, go right on upstairs. If you just want to wash your hands, you can wash up in the kitchen sink. "Now hurry along. The meat loaf is perfect and the baked potatoes are waiting for a dollop of butter. I fried some of the corn I canned last summer and everything is ready—now!"

Sunshine and Fritzy darted into the house and up the stairs. As Adam went in and started for the kitchen, he heard the girls sing out, "Hi Catherine." He wondered what it would be like to have people around him all of the time, no hayloft to slip off to, no woods to stroll through and no orchard to sit in and watch the fruit ripen. Just chatter all of the time. He smiled. Home was full of laughter when his grandparents were still living in the house with him, Pops and Moms. Then, they died; the Army drafted Pops; Moms went to the hospital and Adam was alone in the farm house until the coal ran out. That's when he snuck into town and lived in the church belfry where he would listen to people come and go in the rooms below, making plans for the Christmas bazaar, Sunday dinners and singing in four-part harmony on Thursday evenings at choir practice. He smiled as he washed his hands with Lux. Even the bubbles reminded him of home.

Grace went to the oven and checked the meat loaf again. "It can wait a minute. Before you sit down to eat, Adam, Sergeant Smith wants you to call him when you get in. Give him a quick call. His number is there by the phone."

Adam went back into the living room and dialed the number Grace had left by the telephone.

"Calling your girlfriend?" Shine asked as she whizzed past him on the stairs.

"No," Adam grinned at Fritzy who followed Shine down, and winked.

"Hello?" Adam heard a voice on the other end of the line and turned his attention to the call. Still, he couldn't take his eyes off Fritzy as she walked past him. Had he never really seen her before? He felt serious and giddy all at the same time.

"Hi Sergeant," Adam spoke into the phone. They talked for a minute and Adam gave him a complete after-mission report: about the Trumbulls, their farm, the other men there, the entire invasion by Kruger and Turner and the successful stand-off with the help of Buddy and Freddy.

"And, your dad? Was it really him?" Smith asked.

"Yes," Adam paused as he felt his voice tighten up. He coughed and cleared his throat. "It was Pops. The shock of Kruger and Turner's guns pointed at all of us shook his memory and he remembered me. He has years to catch up on but I'm taking him home."

Adam and Sergeant Smith said their goodbyes and Adam made one more quick call. "Mr. G.?" he spoke into the receiver. "This is Adam."

"My boy, it's good to hear from you. Pastor Bob called and told us you found your father," Alfred Gunderman explained. "Are you able to bring him home?"

"Yes, sir. He's coming back to us slowly but he seems happy," Adam said as he saw everyone gather around the dining room table in the next room. "Can't talk long. I want to ask a favor."

"Anything, Adam," Mr. G. agreed.

"I'd like you and Mrs. G. to take Moms out to the farm," Adam explained. "I think Pops would feel more comfortable there for his first time back in Middletown."

"Absolutely, Adam. Will do."

● ● ●

Adam was stabbing the last piece of his meatloaf with his fork when he saw Mr. Sullivan check the clock on the wall again. Adam knew the time was getting close. He could feel it in some internal clock with which Shaddi had blessed him.

He smiled to himself as he thought about Pops' conversations with him as a child. How he'd told him that God was **El Shaddai, but Adam had only remembered Shaddi.** With his plate clean and his knife and fork placed cross the top, he leaned his elbows on the table and folded his hands. His eyes scanned every face around him. They were all special in so many ways.

Adam smiled again and remembered the last day of school before break. Buddy and Freddy had shoved and pushed younger kids off the sidewalk without so much as an, "Excuse me." Now, just a few days later, who knew that two of the most worthless do-nothings like those two, would throw themselves into the fight at the Trumbull farm, and finally start to grow up?

And Fritzy? He had known her since early elementary school. They were together most of the time, but things were different now. He felt so full and happy when he was around her. Another strange thing—whenever he looked across the table at Fritzy, her warm eyes made Adam's face heat up. That never happened before.

The Sullivans were new friends but friends never-the-less. They reminded him of the people in his church back home, generous, loyal, kind and loving. He would never forget Sunshine, Grace and Dan, and all they shared out of the little they had. But, no one told them that they didn't have enough because they measured enough in love not in things.

Then there was Pops. He looked thin and gaunt but his eyes where shining every time he glanced in Adam's direction. How was it possible that Pops was on his way home after the war, the POW camp, the VA hospital and the scuffle at Trumbull's farm?

Dan stood up, picked up his plate and coffee cup and announced, "It's six o'clock, Adam." As he started into the kitchen; the others silently followed behind.

Adam felt the silence in the kitchen was awkward. They were all standing a little closer, touching a little more and saying their good-byes through the contact of their skin, rather than with their words. As Adam, Will and Fritzy walked outside and got into the cab of the Schumacher farm truck, Buddy hopped into his jalopy while Freddy piled into the passenger seat.

Sunshine yelled from the porch, "Write to me as soon as you get back. Let me know every detail."

"I will," Fritzy sang back.

"You call me, Adam Schumacher," Grace called out as she wiped a tear from her eyes. "I need to know if you all get home okay."

Dan put his arm on Grace's shoulder. "Reverse the charges."

Adam smiled and wondered if he would be able to do such a thing, to make a call and ask the one he called to pay for it. He put the key in the ignition and started the engine. They were going home.

Chapter 29
Will Remembers

A red, white and blue SOHIO sign glistened above two gas pumps up ahead. "I'm going to stop," Adam announced as he pulled up beside pump one, leaving room for Buddy to park by pump two. "Anyone who wants to use the restroom or buy some candy, now's the time."

"Looks like Buddy Phillips is going to top off his tank too," Will said as he got out and stretched his legs.

Adam watched Buddy count the coins in his pockets. "He won't 'top it off.' He'll give the furnace a half shovel of coal." Adam removed the gas cap and inserted the hose. "Pops, you always said it doesn't cost any more to fill up the top half of the tank than it does to fill up the bottom half. The difference is perhaps walking to the next gas station."

"I'm going to look for a candy bar," Fritzy announced. "It's another hour or more until we get to Middletown. "I'll get us each a Butterfinger. If you want something else, speak now or forever hold your order," she sang out as she hurried into the little service station office.

"She's special, son," Will said as he watched Fritzy walk across the station drive.

Adam smiled a silly smile he couldn't seem to control. "I know, Pops."

Will turned to Freddy who had also gotten out and was wiggling his legs as he strutted about. "Are you getting stiff?" Will asked.

"Charley horses," Freddy complained as he walked them off.

Will watched him walk around a little and then suggested, "Sometimes, inside a POW camp, a prisoner would be put in a four by four foot box for punishment. Not able to stand up, his leg cramps would be terrible. I soon discovered, if I pulled my toes back, I could relax the tight, spastic muscles."

"You were a POW?" Freddy asked, his mouth open in amazement.

"Yes, I was," Will said and then quickly changed the subject. "How is your father?"

"You remember my dad?" Freddy's lip curled up in curiosity.

Will smiled and patted the boy's shoulder. "Your dad, Harold, and Buddy's father, Paul and I were classmates. Your father was a good friend. We were on the basketball team together."

Freddy's jaw dropped. "Dad played basketball?"

Will laughed. "He sure did. You didn't know that? He never told you?"

Freddy stared at the ground and shoved his hands in his pockets. "Dad and I don't talk very much. He sells insurance and works long hours." Freddy jingled the change in his pockets. "He said he works slower, so he has to work longer."

Will shook his head. "Everything I had known in the past seems to be flooding back into my memory. That heart valve problem your dad had and the murmur it caused is what took him off the basketball team and kept him out of the service."

"It did?" Freddy asked and exhaled deeply. "I never knew. Thank you Mr. Schumacher—I'm glad to know what happened."

"I imagine he works slowly because of his heart. He probably has to rest a lot during the day, so he has to work longer—slower and longer." Will smiled and nodded.

"And, Buddy's dad?" Freddy asked. "Buddy just said his dad was gone every weekend to get away from him so Buddy stayed away from the house."

"Paul Phillips?" Will asked. "Sure...I do remember him." He looked over at Buddy as he pumped his few gallons of gas.

"Why didn't Mr. Phillips go into the war? Most everyone else did," Freddy asked.

"Don't any of you talk?" Will asked as his eyes shifted from Freddy to Buddy.

"Buddy and I are gone most of the time, around town...you know." Freddy avoided Will's gaze and Will noticed.

"I'm back," Fritzy sang out as she tossed two Butterfingers to Freddy and Buddy. "Don't thank me, Freddy." She said as she reached for the truck door handle. "I don't think I could take the shock."

The smell of gasoline filled the air as Adam removed the nozzle from the truck and twisted the cap back into place. Nodding at Pops, he headed toward the office to pay his bill.

"Paul Phillips?" Will asked again. "Paul was a good guy and a good friend. He came out to all the games and school activities, just like the rest of us. Sometimes he'd stop and pick me up, which I appreciated. His dad had a Model T, and he'd let Paul drive it to evening school activities."

"A Model T?" Freddy asked as he put his hand over his mouth.

"Yup, a Model T." Will turned as Adam came out again. He touched Freddy's arm. "Just one more thing. One night, on his way back from the school, an Amish family in a horse and buggy swerved to miss a deer, causing Paul to jerk the steering wheel hard to the right. He plowed into a huge tree. Paul was in the hospital a long time. They didn't think he'd ever walk again and when he did, he limped. He couldn't pass the Army physical but he wanted to serve. So, they had Paul drive into Chicago and work in a hospital every weekend. That's why he was never home."

Freddy looked stunned. His shoulders were slumped and his eyes focused on nothing in particular.

Adam and Will got in from opposite sides of the Diamond T, each sliding in beside Fritzy. She handed Adam and his dad a Butterfinger and then pealed back the wrapper on her own bar. "Umm," she sighed and closed her eyes as she took a bite of the candy.

"These are great," Will agreed. "I haven't had one of these in…years." He took another bite and, picking at his shirt, he nibbled up the crispy crumbs that fell there.

"Dad," Adam began and then looked past Fritzy at the next stoplight to see Pops more closely. "You are remembering things so fast. Moms will be so excited."

"She's been through a lot," Will whispered as he looked out the side window to the darkening fields beyond. He cleared his throat and added, "It looks like the farmer on this side of the road has the tilling and planting done already this spring."

"The rows are straight;" Adam joined in, "just like you would have planted them, Pops." He was aware that his dad changed the topic again. He wondered if his father would always run from hard conversations. He hadn't in the past. But, Pops had fought in a war and survived a POW camp since he left Indiana over three years ago. Adam decided to meet his dad head on. "Yep, Moms was really sick. But, she went to a T.B. sanitarium and they took real good care of her."

"But," Will started to say, choking on his words. "I should have been here to take care of her."

"Pops, POW's can't just get a hall pass to come home when they're needed." Adam waited. How much should he say? How much should he ask?

"What about your grandma and grandpa? How are they doing?" Will asked.

"You don't know about them?" Oh no. Adam thought the Red Cross had contacted Pops. The accident happened before the Battle of the Bulge.

"I..." Will rubbed his forehead and eyebrows. "I don't know." He closed his eyes and rubbed harder. "Oh..." he gasped. "Yes, someone called me into the officer's tent." His eyes fixed on the oncoming headlights, like he was in a hypnotic trance. He shook his head and rubbed his eyes again. "Yes, they told me. I want to forget it...like it never happened. But, if I do, I may forget everyone again...even me."

"I'm really glad you know who you are, Pops," Adam said while Fritzy sat between them and said nothing. "And, I'm glad you remember the rest of us."

"Me, too," Will agreed. "Me, too."

Chapter 30
Home

A full golden moon hung above the woods at the back of the Schumacher farm as the Diamond T pulled into the lane. Buddy drove his old junker in behind it and followed Adam down toward the house. Adam had told the two boys they could stop in, get a drink of water and use the bathroom before driving on into town.

Adam had been holding a silent argument with himself for miles. What was he thinking? Why did he believe Pops' homecoming should be at the farm? No one had lived in the house for over seven months. He and Fritzy had gone out beyond the lights of the city and dusted the place a few times. And, every time they had opened the front door, stale air hit their senses in full assault. His parents' reunion should be warm and cozy, rather than with the insult of cobwebs in the corners and dust bunnies under the chairs.

"What's all of this?" Fritzy asked as they approached the white frame farm house. The porch light was gleaming, a homing beacon with amber lights glowed from every window. Parked cars lined the lane, half on the gravel and half in the grass. "There have to be about twenty cars lined up along here," Fritzy gasped.

"I have no idea what this is all about." Adam looked into every car as they passed but each was empty. "I hope there's nothing wrong with Moms."

"Has she been feeling bad again?" Will asked. His voice cracked a little with concern. "You just talked to her again this afternoon, before we left Ohio. Did she sound weak or sick?"

"She was fine when I left on Saturday, and she sounded the same this afternoon," Adam said as he shook his head. "Mr. Gunderman would have called me before we left Beavertown if she had gotten sick."

"Alfred?" Will asked as the corners of his mouth turned up and his eyes brightened. "I remember him."

Adam nearly leaped straight up as he clung to the steering wheel. "That's great, Pops! You really remember Mr. G.?"

"Sure do," Will spoke out with confidence. "He was the head janitor at Middletown High School when I went there. The Vice-Principal sent out-of-control boys to the basement to help Mr. Gunderman. Alfred would ask the kids to help him read better but they could only use the Bible to teach him. Many a boy turned their life around because of the time they spent with Alfred."

"I didn't know that Pops," Adam breathed out slowly and thought about all the times he had spent with Mr. G. *Thanks Shaddi,* he prayed silently.

"Look," Fritzy pointed to a vehicle parked to the side of the lane. "That's my parents' car!"

"Coach's car?" Adam asked as he looked again. "But, what would it be doing here?"

"I ought to know my own parents' car," she spit out. "Besides, Daddy has been teaching me to drive in that car."

"You're learning to drive?" Adam asked as he tried to turn and look directly at Fritzy sitting beside him. Why didn't he know she had been all over town behind her dad's steering wheel?

"What?" she snapped. "Because I'm a girl, I can't drive?" She shook her head and added, "You really are a Neanderthal, aren't you, Adam Schumacher?"

There she goes again, Adam thought. He was learning to be wiser about not saying everything he knew out loud. He couldn't understand the come-here/go-away, yoyo type of relationship his friendship with Fritzy had turned into. "Neanderthal? No," Adam tried to joke. "I ah...just hadn't seen you driving around town. Thought a dinosaur was your preferred mode of transportation." *Oops. Adam, keep your thoughts to yourself.*

"Don't be silly," she scolded. "A dinosaur would make too much of a mess in the school parking lot." She masked a little laugh by covering her mouth with her hand. "Besides, that's okay, Adam Schumacher. I don't need your permission to drive," she stated flatly and folded her arms. "I know what I know without confirmation from other people."

Will patted Fritzy on the knee, a silent warning he was changing the subject—fast. "Somebody brought the old tractor out of the barn," he pointed to the middle of the barnyard. "It looks like someone has recently plowed the fields. Wow. I have a head start on planting."

There was an empty parking spot beside the sidewalk that led up to the front door. Adam pulled the truck to a stop and turned off the engine. In spite of all the cars parked along the lane, no one was around. The porch was empty but Adam could see that the front door was open. The screen door awaited entry. "Fritzy, we did close that front door when we left the last time, didn't we?"

"We definitely did," she agreed.

Suddenly, there was no sound inside the car or outside, except for the excited breathing of all three of them. They looked at the house for a few seconds but remained fixed.

"Well, I'm getting out," Fritzy stated finally. "One of you will have to move," she insisted and started leaning in Will's direction, as though she expected him to get out of her way.

"Yes, Ma'am," Will said and laughed. "Yep, you have some girl there, son." He put his hand on the door and started to open it when Adam jumped down from the truck on the driver's side.

Adam's first reaction was to say, "I don't own her. She's her own boss." But, he got smart about girls in a hurry—his girl in particular. So, he said nothing, but smiled.

Adam took the lead up to the door. He didn't know what to expect, and he wanted to shield Pops from any disappointment or shock. A faint whiff of something sweet floated through the screen door. Will stood back and let Fritzy follow Adam, although it was obvious from the wringing of his hands that he was anxious to get in his own house—his home.

Inside, the living room was clean and dusted. A large clear crystal vase of flowers sat on the mantle. Since it was early in the spring and only a few flowers were in bloom, it was obvious to Adam they were an expensive bouquet from a florist shop. They smelled wonderful, but it still wasn't the sweetness Adam had noticed. He looked around the room but saw no one.

To the left of the parlor, a large case opening led into the dining room. That was it, the origin of the sweet aroma. A white lace tablecloth covered the surface. Moms didn't own lace anything. Then, Adam remembered. Last Christmas, Fritzy invited him to her grandparents' home for dinner. Mrs. Stafford had placed a lace tablecloth under the dinner plates on her table. And, it looked exactly like the one on the table there in his farm house. He looked at Fritzy, grinned and shrugged—his arms out and palms up.

"That's Grandma Stafford's table cloth," Fritzy whispered. "I know it is. See the border of large S's tatted into the edge?"

The table was loaded with platters of hot sliced turkey that smelled like Thanksgiving in the spring and rich browned roast beef. A huge crystal glass bowl full of potato salad with the savory perfume of sweet onions, and the tangy aroma of chopped pickles anchored one corner. Someone artfully placed a large basket of yeasty smelling rolls between the meat platters and circled it with smaller dishes of mayonnaise, mustard, horseradish and catsup. A large assortment of cheese and colorful crisp vegetables graced Grandma Schumacher's Haviland china serving plate. One end of the table held a cut glass punch bowl and at the other end a silver coffee service, complete with cream pitcher and sugar bowl.

"Wow," Adam breathed out slowly. "Who? How?"

"I don't know who," Will began as tears came to his eyes. "But, it looks wonderful."

"Surprise!" Reverend Silverman rang out as he came in from the kitchen followed by what looked to Adam like half the town.

"Welcome home!" All the people cheered as they swarmed into the dining room.

Beatrice Bianca Brumble was the first to shake Will's hand. "I am so glad you are finally home with your loved ones," B.B said as she smiled.

"Thanks B.B." Will choked and rubbed his eyes.

Adam's heart raced as he watched friends and neighbors greet his father on his return. He had no idea that so many people even knew Pops was gone. What thrilled him more than anything was that Pops actually seemed to know most of the people who filled his home.

Connie Silverman smiled at Adam as she came in. "Hi Adam. I'm so glad you were able to bring your dad home." She took a small box of wooden matches from her pocket, removed one and struck it on the side of the box, then lit the candles on the table. The flame filled the room with a warm glow. It danced in the happy eyes of all those who came out of the kitchen clapping and laughing.

"I don't think I know this lady," Will said to Adam as Connie poured a cup of punch for him.

"I'm sorry," Adam apologized. "Pops, this is Reverend Silverman's wife, Connie."

Will offered his hand in friendship. "You're part of the church that took care of my son when I was gone."

"Yes, sir," she said as she smiled. "It was a joy to do so. And, Adam took care of us."

Freddy came into the room slowly, his head down which gave away his discomfort. That is, until he saw his father behind the Silvermans. "Dad," he stammered. "What are you doing here?"

Harold Alexander reached out his hand to Will. "The whole city will be dropping by this evening, son," he said as he shook Will's hand. "I wanted to welcome a friend home."

"Harold..." Will greeted with a chuckle and embraced his old friend. "Is Bonnie with you?"

"You know my mother, too?" Freddy asked.

"I do," Will answered as Harold's wife stepped forward.

Will gave Carol Alexander a friendly hug and turned to Freddy. "You have great parents, Freddy."

Freddy shuffled his feet back and forth on the floor, smiled sheepishly and nodded.

Everyone was there. Coach and Mrs. Bremen even brought Fitzy's older brother, Jimmy, a college student home for Easter break. Both Willard and Alma Stafford not only came, they paid for a lot of the food. Adam always liked them.

"Adam," Willard vigorously patted Adam on the back, "Alma and I can never thank you enough for getting rid of those—unwelcomed guests in our basement before last Christmas' party at our house." He winked and thumped him some more.

Fritzy giggled, cupped her hand over her mouth and whispered, "My grandparents would never want to hear the word 'rat' spoken in association with their fine home."

Adam threw his head back and laughed. "I'm glad I was able to help."

Mrs. Brubaker, Adam's English teacher came with her husband and Mr. Humphrey came with his wife.

"Adam," Mr. Humphrey said as he extended his hand, "you're no longer a boy. You have proven yourself to be a young man. I said you could do it—and you did. You found your dad and brought him home."

Adam's diaphragm quivered as his tears ran inside, tears he refused to shed for others to see. He stiffened his spine and stood up even taller.

Will greeted Buddy's parents with a hearty hand shake. "Paul," he said as he reached over his friend's shoulder and clapped him heartily. "It is so good to see you my friend."

Buddy's eyes darted back and forth. Perhaps he was afraid someone had seen Will Schumacher show friendship to his dad. Everyone in the room knew that Buddy had no idea how to make a friend. He looked at Adam and smiled faintly.

Kathy Breman brought in a plate of snickerdoodle cookies, the sugar and cinnamon perfume filled Adam with joy. She put the little treats on the table and wrapped her arms around Fritzy. "Frederica, I am so glad you two are home." She stood back and smiled.

"Mama, I'm glad we're home, too," Fritzy said as she reached for her dad.

Coach James Breman beamed all over. "Honey, we are so proud of you. Dragged into things way over your heads, you handled yourselves like adults." He turned to Adam and let out a hoot. "Young man," he called out, "come over here and let me shake your hand."

Adam didn't hesitate. Finally treated as an adult, he needed to savor the moment. "Thank you for coming, Coach. I know Pops is happy everyone is here."

"James," Will reached out his hand, "thank you for coming. And, thanks for sharing your daughter. She's quite a little lady."

Kathy and James Breman smiled. "We'll have many days to hear all about your time in Ohio. Right now, welcome home."

"Thank you two," Will said with a wide smile.

"Thanks," Adam said and looked at Fritzy. She knew what they had been through and she stood beside him. He looked around at all those who had come so far. Even Charlie Baker brought Barbara James to the great celebration. Adam smiled when he remembered his mornings in the cold bell tower when Charlie would pull up in front of Barbara's house, sound his ahooga horn and wait to take her to school. It was Adam's wake-up call, too.

Sidney Crammer, the farmer next door, was the last one out of the kitchen. He came in clean coveralls and his wife was in a new cotton flowered house dress. Sidney smiled quietly and shook Will's hand with the power of someone who works with his hands all day.

Adam looked around at the smiles on all the faces there in the room. But, Moms wasn't there.

"I hope your mother's all right," Will said as he scanned all the familiar faces, anxious and wringing his hands again.

"Connie," Adam finally asked, "where is my mother? Pops has waited a long time to see her."

"Arletta called right before we left the parsonage" she said as she watched Will. "She said Bridget was so excited she collapsed and…"

"Collapsed?" Will and Adam gasped at the same moment.

"Just nervous exhaustion," Connie insisted. "She took a nap and was just waking up when Arletta called. She's feeling better and will be here in a few minutes."

"That's jake," Adam said, relieved.

Will began to pace, thumping the fingertips of one hand on the top of the other. The twitching of Pops eyes was hard for Adam to watch.

"Pops, she's okay," he stated confidently. "I know she is. She's just so excited it wore her out a little. She rested, and she'll be here, soon."

"I know, but…but," Will's word stumbled and stopped before he could spit them out and fear crept into his eyes.

"It'll be okay, Pops," Adam began, and then paused when he heard the screen door bang. Adam was relieved to see his mother come in, followed by Arletta and Alfred Gunderman. Adam's eyes darted to Pops, hoping his father would be able to withstand the excitement. Proudly and with a full measure of jitters, Adam went to the door, took his mother by the arm and helped her into the living room.

"Adam," Bridget whispered with a voice weak but full of hope, "you brought him home to us, just like you said you would. I am so proud of you."

Everyone fixed on Adam, Bridget and Will. Their eyes, as they gazed on each other, shone with love and the promise of hope and healing. Their center was everyone's center that evening. Some friends had tears in their eyes; all were overflowing with giddy joy. Adam knew, because they were all silent. Yet the words they would have spoken, if the scene weren't so precious, hung heavy in the room.

"Briggy," Will said as his voice choked, and he fought back his own tears.

Adam had never heard Pops call Moms Briggy before. Adam blushed. It was a little like "Fritzy," his name for Frederica.

Will walked slowly over to his wife and, gathering Bridget in his arms, he drew her to him. Kissing her tenderly, he then turned and grabbed Adam into one large family embrace.

"I can't believe you're finally home, Will," Bridget murmured as she buried her head in his shoulder. With happy tears in her eyes she added, "And we owe it all to you, son."

Adam's tears finally rolled down his face and dripped off his chin. He wiped them quickly on his sleeve. All those gathered there shed their own tears of joy.

Adam watched Fritzy. Her eyes glistened when she saw Will embrace Adam's mother for the first time in too many years.

Pops was home but Adam was aware his thoughts had shifted. All he could think about now was hugging the prettiest girl in the room. When did everything change? It wasn't in a flash—or maybe it was. Adam reached for Fritzy's hand that slipped into his like he had been holding her hand for years. "I'll pick you up for the Spring Fling at seven—if that's okay with you?"

"It's perfect," Fritzy whispered. "Just like this Easter break has been perfect."

Adam watched the light in Pops eyes burn brighter and brighter. "Perfect," he whispered.

Epilogue

Adam knew the Spring Fling would be a great party; it would be the best Easter ever. He had helped to heal his broken family and had gotten a girlfriend at the same time. Looking around, the shadows were gone. Not a single one remained.

Like when he retrieved the stolen Christ Child carving at Christmas, Adam had been brave enough to go into danger and find his father. He believed that Pops had died, but Adam was courageous enough to walk into the line of fire and bring him home again. His best friend had turned into much more, and his family had received grace and was born again. Adam knew; he had found timeless joy and the Nectar of Life.

Blessed People from my Past

While this is a work of fiction, there are some exceptions, such as the names of streets and some buildings in the Dayton area. The Reference section contains an article that details the Manhattan Project in the Dayton area during WWII. If I have described something incorrectly, forgive me as my memory may get it wrong.

Beavertown Evangelical United Brethren Church is also real. Now called Church of the Cross United Methodist in Kettering, Ohio (old Beavertown), is also full of blessed past images. I grieve for those who do not have the music and people of their childhood place-of-worship to lean on in times of need. My visit to the church's archives brought back the names of dear saints from my past: people like my parents, Dan and Mildred Gaines and my aunt and uncle, Ollie and Menford Hattery. Also there were pillars of the church: our pastor, Dr. E.R. Turner, Harold and Julia Delaney, Gaylord and Nell Alspach, Ray and Evelyn Puckett, Bob Orth, Orlo Medsger and his daughter Barbara, Carl and Millie Chandelier, Charles and Anna Funk, Charles and Opel Mendenhall, Preston and Reba Scott, Maurice and Louise Wogaman, Clarence and Bessie Watkins, Esther Welde, Henry Becker—who ushered every Sunday, and Clyde Roberts' wife, Annette who taught the Travels of Paul, to my sixth grade Sunday School class, as if her best friend had just gotten back from a dangerous trip and she couldn't wait to tell everybody about it. I saw all the precious ladies of the church in Mrs. Garver's service of hot cross buns.

Daniel Sullivan, modeled after my father, Daniel M. Gaines, tells Daddy's backstory and my mother Mildred M. Gaines, as Grace, did not like gardening although her mother, my grandmother, Bertha Bryson was president of the Gardening Club in Greenville, Ohio. I grew up in Sullivan's house and my memories of my home are sweet. Yes, my parents let me travel all over Dayton, wherever the bus and trolley system could take me. I particularly remember the Dayton Arcade and Saturday morning movies at the NCR auditorium.

Reference

https://en.wikipedia.org/wiki/Dayton_Project. Dayton Project. (Part of the Manhattan Project to build the first Atomic bomb.) Accessed 10/26/2016.

OTHER BOOKS BY DORIS GAINES RAPP

Novelette:

News at Eleven (Glo Magazine - Serialized Jan, Feb, March, and April 2015 Expanded to:

News at Eleven – A Novel (Released April 2015)

Novels:

Length of Days – The Age of Silence

Length of Days – Beyond the Valley of the Keepers

Length of Days – Search for Freedom

Escape from the Belfry

Smoke from Distant Fires

Hiawassee – Child of the Meadow

News at Eleven – A Novel

Collection:

Christmas Feathers, one of eight short stories in a wonderful collection titled, **Christmases Past**

Children's:

Lincoln's Christmas Mouse

Non-Fiction:

Waiting for Jesus in a Can't Wait World – Advent 2014

Prayer Therapy of Jesus

Promote Yourself

Internet Presence:

www.prayertherapyrapp.blogspot.com

www.dorisgainesrapp.blogspot.com

Website: www.dorisgainesrapp.com

Facebook: Doris Gaines Rapp – Author Page

About the Author

Doris Gaines Rapp, Ph.D. is a writer by birth, psychologist and teacher by education and experiences. She creates fictional characters that live in several centuries and loves the stories she tells. As a psychologist, she understands the people who appear on her computer screen; she laughs with them, cries with them, and triumphs over adversity with them. They are real and full of life. All of her works have at their heart a Christian world view.

Rapp also writes on the non-fiction topics of self-publishing with an encouragement to promote yourself and your work; as well as Prayer Therapy, learning to pray specifically so God can answer prayers specifically.

She speaks on several topics:

Voices of Assertiveness within My Novels

Write About What You Know

Prayer Therapy

Promote Yourself

Know Your Own History

Live All of Your Life

Step Out of Your Comfort Zone

Dr. Rapp is a former counseling center director of Taylor University, Upland, IN and Bethel College, Mishawaka, IN. She currently writes and speaks full time. She and her pastor husband have survived rearing six children. They live in Indiana.